#Cursed

J.J Ems

Contents

This book is dedicated to anyone and everyone who has ever felt
misunderstood, out of place, or just plain different.

We are all universally connected.

You are loved.

CHAPTER ONE

Lexie

IT'S FUNNY HOW PEOPLE wonder when, or if, time travel will ever exist because to me, I already experience it. As I lay back on my front porch and conjure up my usual playlist, I'm instantly transported to days when things were simpler, and I felt less stressed, less pulled from left to right.

The scent in the air helps bring me back to these earlier times, as the smell of fresh-cut grass and burning charcoal brushes across my nose, reminding me of the barbeques we would have as a kid and watching my mom and dad hover over the grill, chuckling, and most likely sharing old memories.

I wonder if I tried hard enough. If I could just go back, just close my eyes and wish, and suddenly I would...

"LEXIIIIII!"

My little sister comes bumbling through the front door with a book in one hand, my purse, and Kenzie, her favorite doll, in the other.

"You almost forgot this!"

She hands me my purse with a grin painted on, clearly proud she saved my day.

"Thanks, Xyla,"

I stuff my purse into my bag and sit up off the staircase of my porch because clearly, she wants to talk.

"Hey Lex, are we still going to have our thriller movie night tonight? I really want to see something with a good twist! You know I'm going to be a detective one day, and I need to know all the possible endings these stories can have!"

"Sure, Xyla, as long as they don't keep me late at work tonight," I say, trying to sound as enthusiastic as possible.

"Don't forget! I'm going to ask mom and dad to get snacks so we can be prepared."

She scurries off, and her little brown bob haircut bounces away through the doorway.

Ugh, what I would give to remember what it's like to have that childlike glee again.

As I lean back to relax back into my trip down memory lane, my time-traveling experience quickly comes to a halt as I realize my Dryve approaching the front gate.

I gather my things, drag my feet sloppily to the car, and greet the driver before I slouch lazily into the rear seat of his hatchback, trying to ignore the pungent odor of what smells like patchouli and sunscreen.

"How's it going today?" he asks. His tone is dry as if he feels this conversation is on his long list of tasks to do for the day, and he's trying hard to plop on that check mark.

"Good, Thanks," I reply, not bothering to ask him how his day is going, saving us both from a drawn-out conversation where we frantically search our brains for the following words to utter in hopes of hanging on to meaningless chatter that will instantaneously dissipate once I exit this vehicle.

With my conversation diversion successful, I reach into my bag and pull out my secret stash.

One of my concealer flasks.

It may seem like an ordinary hairbrush to the untrained eye, but my dear friend Ella has gifted me this convenient on-the-go flask, which now carries my oh-so-delicious cookie dough whiskey with me for almost any occasion.

I look up at the rearview mirror to ensure my driver isn't glancing back at me while I attempt to take this shot.

That's right, Dan, mind your business.

I quickly down my shot of whiskey, pull out my compact, and attempt to fix my hair when I hear a *ping* on my phone.

New Guy Alert!

OMG, really? Cute? Our Dept? I Need Tea.

I'm dying to hear her response, as there hasn't been a new person working in our department for such a long time. It would help as we are clearly all overworked, in my opinion.

ping

suspenseful music…. ha-ha, and that's all you get until you get here! Girl, hurry up!

Yeah, like all the time! Love ya!

I put my phone back in my bag and direct my attention back up to my driver, who seems to be in his own little world, shooting an occasional glance into the backseat.

Oh, the joys of an awkward Dryve ride...

It happens to be a beautiful day, nonetheless.

As the car makes its way through the streets on the way to my hellish job, aka the *Torture Chamber*, I manage to appreciate brief glimpses of nature through the car window.

The beautiful shades of the leaves that have fallen to the ground, the bright blue of the sky, and the light clusters of clouds. I've always loved autumn in Wellwash Springs; it's so magical, so full of possibility.

Now, if only its magic could make my work schedule disappear, then we would be talking about miracles!

I grab my bag as Dan finally pulls up to FURNISH, our all too literal name for the furniture store I currently work at, and I thank him for the lift.

God, I don't want to do this...

I exit his car, pop in a lavender mint, and head my way into my personal hell of a job, all while trying to locate my ID badge to get through the damn door.

When I find my badge, I scan in and proceed through the show-room, dying a little bit inside as I walk through the departments leading to mine.

Living-Rooms, *dying*, Kitchens, *still dying*, Bedrooms, *almost not alive.*Ah! Home Office, *dead inside, fully dead.*

As I make my way through the Home Office showroom, I spot Aella waving, her bedazzled tie shimmering from the many lights in the above fixtures.

She's occupied with a customer at the moment, so I take this time to settle in.

I lay my bag behind the desk at my usual workstation and pop out my Purr Kittie compact to check my makeup really quickly before signing into the work computer.

God, I really need to get more sleep.

I put my compact away and start to log in because I figure there's no escaping the *Torture Chamber* now.

As I'm logging in, I see Aella walking over, and I must admit I'm excited to hear everything about this new guy I strangely haven't spotted since I've walked into the building.

"Hey Lex, Omg! I love the new hair."

I flick my pink braids to the side and bat my eyelashes, giving her the full experience.

"Thanks, Ella, you know, trying something different."

"Yeah, you are always switching it up. I think I should try something new, too."

She twirls her straight red hair in between her fingers, looking up at the ceiling.

"Okay, Ella, fashion drama later. Where's this new guy you told me about? We haven't had a new person around our age here in forever."

"Okay, you've only been working here for a year, and he went on the newbie tour with Jaden. God, do you remember that? Like Hello! We can navigate the building ourselves."

"What's his name?"

"Yohan, but he said his friends call him Yo-Yo. He has a story about it, and I'm sure he'll tell you all about it when you meet him."

She rolls her eyes, and I can't help but chuckle because he seems to be a bit theatrical by her vague description so far.

I can't help but ask more questions.

"But is he cute?"

"Girl, he went on a quick tour of the building, not a vacation. You'll see in a few. My suspenseful music text would be in vain if I didn't let you wait for a little."

"Well, I see my *your extremely annoying* text served its purpose."

She laughs and walks over to a customer who seems impatient.

Honestly, I'm glad she's always so willing to talk to every person who walks up because I'm just settling in, and I'm so not ready to be bombarded with customer questions about desks and chairs or file cabinets.

I pull up my work email to see if I have anything interesting, but nope, just company updates and pats on the back for our all-star employees, which, as always, I am excluded from.

I shift my eyes above my computer screen and notice two guys walking toward the desk, Jaden and this mysterious guy who must be Yohan or Yo-Yo, I guess.

I try not to stare, but I must admit he has something mysterious going on with him.

The blue patch in the front of his curly hair is definitely unique. You don't see much of that from the guys here in WellWash Springs, but also, the tattoos and his carefree walk give him this kind of bad boy vibe that's hard to describe... and suddenly the million-dollar question is answered in my head, yes, he is cute.

Definitely cute.

I try not to look like I'm staring or seem awkward, so I continue to scroll, reading absolutely nothing that is passing along my screen, waiting for them to approach me so Jaden can give his probably rehearsed introduction.

"Hey, Lex,"

"Oh, Hey, Jaden,"

"This is Yohan. He will be training with you guys in Home Offices for the next few days. Can you show him a few of the systems we use here, you know, the basic stuff, to get him started?"

I try not to roll my eyes because, although Jaden is friendly, I find how invested he is in this job to be highly annoying.

"Sure," I respond.

As Jaden walks off, I can sense the awkwardness between me and Yohan attempting to grow, so I quickly try to stir up conversation.

"So, dream job or way to pay the bills?"

I glance at Ella because I can feel her staring and muster up a slight chuckle as I redirect my attention back to Yohan.

"Yeah, definitely not a dream job."

He laughs.

"I actually just moved here and applied to several jobs online, and this is the one I got a reply from, so here I am."

I can't help but notice how calm and mellow his voice is. The mystery factor is skyrocketing. Who is this guy?

"Well, it's not that bad here. Actually, most of the time, we get to hang out and just straighten out the showroom. Apparently, not many people are looking to set up offices in their homes these days, now Bedrooms, that's where the actions at."

He laughs, and I realize my words of choice, but hey, who cares? If he's going to get to know me, he's going to get it authentically.

"Seems about right," he replies.

As the day progresses, I find Yo-Yo to be a perfect fit for the little vibe we have going on here in our department; he and Ella make my day go by quickly as we exchange stories about our teenage years, question each other about our favorite movies, and make plans to hang out after work tomorrow at me and Ella's favorite spot Eat Your Heart Out Bakery.

I exchange numbers with him and head into my Dryve, excited to make my way home.

The Dryve ride was quiet, and I spent most of my time on my phone scrolling through things I want to buy.

I call it Virtual window shopping, and it's my favorite pastime.

God, if I could purchase everything on my list, I swear I would probably be considered a hoarder at this point.

Wait, am I virtually hoarding? Do I have a problem?

The Dryve pulls up to my front gate, and I thank George for the awkward ride and make my way inside.

As soon as I get in, I throw my bag on the bed, reach for my cookie dough whiskey, take a swig, and prop open my laptop.

I head to the job boards and start applying to all the one-click options I see available, not really reading the needed qualifications or job descriptions when I notice a notification pop up on the right side of my screen.

New Message

Invitation To Interview

Thank You for your interest...

Omg already?! Yes, yes, yes. Thank you, universe, I am a master manifester. Yes, yes!

I dance a little in my seat as I click open.

Invitation to Interview

Thank You for your interest in our customer service role here at Astral Connections,

We would like to schedule an interview with you at your earliest convenience. As per protocol, please review the attached documentation for instructions on moving forward with the interview process.

We look forward to hearing from you!

Best Regards.

It seems a bit short and informal, especially with the lack of a name listed after the closing of the email, but hey, who am I to turn down a new job opportunity? Even though my job at *FURNISH* isn't the worst, I could definitely use some additional cash. I need to move out of here and start fresh on my own.

I scroll down and hesitate a bit before clicking the attachment. The last thing I need is a virus taking over my laptop once again, causing me an out-of-pocket expense I certainly cannot afford.

Girl, what are you waiting for?

I click open on the attachment.

Aidens Spiral

**Used for protection, symbolizes protec-
tion by fire. Can protect an individual
from……**

……………

Simple Wishing
**Chanting holds power simply by chanting
wishes with pure intent……**

……………

What the hell is this?

I continue scrolling, taking in bits and pieces of information. Whatever the hell it is, it's not job-related, and I don't think it was meant for me.

I don't know if it's the whiskey kicking in, but I can't help but continue to scroll through, scanning through random lines of the included text, trying to figure out what the hell I am reading.

****Warning*****
**Words hold power. Choose your words care-
fully as they can affect…**

…………

**You are more powerful than you think the
universe can assist you…**

……………

YOU HAVE BEEN CHOSEN

No, I have not.

"You got the wrong one."

I suddenly feel nauseous. That was a lot to take in. I quickly delete the email and try to wrap my head around what I just saw.

Was it witchcraft? It definitely seemed occult-y, and I have been chosen?

It has to be a mistake, some scam, or junk mail, or some nerd having fun behind his computer screen thinking he can play games with unknowing victims.

Yeah, that's it. It definitely has to be nerd games.

But then it hits me, that image, Aiden's Spiral. Where have I seen that before?

I'm frantically searching my brain, like there's a mini-me running through all the file cabinets of my memories, opening drawer after drawer, trying to find the answer.

Then, it finally clicks.

Yohan.

Yohan has that tattoo.

KNOCK *KNOCK*

"Lexi, are you ready to watch the movie yet? I can start the popcorn, and I got Mom and Dad to get your favorite pretzels from the store."

I quickly close my laptop and swivel my desk chair to face the door where my little sister is peering her head in, anticipating my answer, full of energy as always.

"Yes, I'll be right there. Let me just change, and it's mystery movie time," I say, putting on my best impersonation of one of those voice-over commercial guys.

"Yay," she replies, closing the door, and I can hear her shoes skipping down the hall.

I take one more swig of my cookie dough whiskey, quickly change, and grab my phone as I get ready to head to the living room and have movie night with Xyla.

As I place my hand on the doorknob to exit the room, I can't help but think.

I'm on to you, Mr. Yo-Yo.

Your mysterious vibes won't last long, especially not when you decide to play around with a girl like me.

CHAPTER TWO

Yohan

♫ ♫ ♫ *"Shut the system down, Shut it down, Shut it down, Shut the system down. They don't deserve to make a sound."* ♫ ♫ ♫

♫ ♫ ♫ *"I GET WRECKLESS, I GET WRECKLESS!"* ♫ ♫ ♫

** KNOCK KNOCK KNOCK**

I turn the music down and pause my sketching, which I hate to do when I'm fully engaged. It throws me off, and I feel the finished product is never really the same, but I guess I'm being summoned by my dad, and by the sound of his heavy knocking, I'm in for it.

My dad opens the door and pops his head in through the frame with an obviously irritated look illustrated on his face.

"Really Yohan? Does it have to be that loud, and how can you even understand what they're saying? It just sounds like screaming!"

"You have to listen, Pa, there's actually meaning..."

I stop myself because I realize I've tried to convince him of this several times before, and by the impatient way he's repeatedly tapping his foot, I'm coerced to save us both the trouble.

He looks down and slows his breathing, clearly trying to calm himself down, and it is at that very moment I begin to feel one of those stern *"get your life together"* speeches becoming the essence of our impending conversation.

"Yohan, you are Twenty-Two."

"Of this, I am aware," I say, instantly regretting it.

"Yohan!"

"Sorry, Pa. I'm Twenty-Two, go on."

"Lord help me." He sighs. "How was your first day on the new job?"

"Just like every other, I mean, my coworkers seem cool, like let's be honest here, I'm working at a furniture store in the middle of nowhere selling office equipment, so nothing special. A girl asked me if it was my dream job, and I said no, and yeah, that pretty much sums it up."

"See, Yohan, if you had chosen college, you would have had more options. You wouldn't be moving with me from place to place because of my job. I know you get tired of it and will eventually want to settle down, you know, get a place of your own."

I don't know why, but something about what he's saying makes my skin itch. The sarcasm almost wants to rush out of my lips instantly, but I hold back. I can't say what I want to say, and what I want to say is, "Is that what I want? Or is that what you want? Freedom?"

I refrain.

"Pa, I'm working on it. I just haven't found my thing yet, and once I do, I'll be on my own, and it'll be soon, I promise."

Damnit, Yohan, not the correct response.

I can see his face become sullen like he feels like he said the wrong thing. My dad is not a bad guy, and sometimes, I regret my word choice or tone when having serious conversations like this with him. He tries his best to be a good father, but I can tell he's sensitive on the inside and that gene has obviously carried over.

"I didn't mean it like that, Yohan, and you know that. I want to see you happy, that's all."

"I know Pa."

He glances over to look at my sketchbook and raises an eyebrow.

He chuckles.

"Nice sketch, one of your fantasy creatures again, I see. I'm surprised you didn't turn out to be one of those guys obsessed with those board games with the weird dice."

"There's still time, Pa, nothing but time," I laugh.

He chuckles again and begins to back his head out of the doorway.

"All right, well, I'll leave you to it."

"Oh, and by the way, in case you get hungry, I left some empanadas out for you so you can grab a bite before work."

"Thanks, Dad."

He shuts the door, and I close my sketchbook, just feeling like I've lost inspiration.

Guess my muses weren't wanting to have that conversation....

I check my watch and realize I still have some time to kill before I have to get ready to head to work, so I grab my Cannapuffy, take a few hits, and consider grabbing that book I bought on the power of symbolism and giving it another try.

Yeah... Not in the mood for that.

I reach for my laptop instead and sign into my messenger, hoping that my buddy Bash is online because, out of all the people I've met, journeying from place to place, he is definitely my person.

This guy gets me.

I see the little green circle lit up with life next to his screen name: ColorSplozion83. I double-click the icon, and when the chat box opens, I type a quick message:

ItzYoYo: An unannounced visitor has arrived.

I see the dots dancing on the screen.

ColorSplozion83: YoYo! It's always lovely to have you, could've at least called ahead. The place is a mess. #WarnABitchNextTime.

ItzYoYo: lol will do, what's up?

ColorSplozion83: You know, the usual, trying to slay the beast I call boredom but failing… miserably.

ItzYoYo: Ugh, tell me about it.

ColorSplozion83: So, are you a furniture expert yet? I'm thinking about getting a new desk, and I need the kind you don't have to put together because I already know that will be a failure. Lol.

I can't help but laugh. See this, this is what I needed.

ItzYoYo: Yeah, I can just picture your lopsided worktable now, lol, but honestly, I don't even really know what options we have yet, but I'll get back to you on that.

ItzYoYo: What about you? How was your day?

ColorSplozion83: If I'm being honest, my day kind of royally sucked, but way too much to type…

I begin to click aimlessly on the keyboard, somewhere falling between randomly typing, erasing words, and nonsensically smashing letters to give the illusion that I am trying hard to find the right thing to say.

But am I trying? Or am I really lost? He's usually the hero. I'm just waiting to be rescued, always waiting to be rescued.

The selfish part of me gets slightly agitated because my intention was for Bash to distract me from feeling like I spent twenty-two years of my life accomplishing absolutely nothing. Still, the other part of me feels like he needs a friend right now, and after everything we've been through, I know I owe him at least that.

ItzYoYo: VChat?

Almost instantly, I see a request to connect via webcam pop up on my screen. I give it a few seconds and click accept.

"Wow, you weren't kidding. Your room really is a mess," I say jokingly.

He dryly chuckles.

His energy does not match the words that were populating on my screen a minute ago, and he seems to be staring down from the camera awkwardly from time to time, it's very unlike him.

Still, more importantly, I notice something different: something is missing.

"I haven't seen you without make-up for years. Did you fire your glam squad? Or, let me guess, waiting for one of those new collector's edition palettes?" I tease.

"Yeah, I'm giving that up." He says, tone dry and despondent.

"What? Why?"

"I dunno, I just am. It's just hard."

He shifts his hand to his head and clenches his long, curly hair with his fist. I can see the emotion building up in him through his wavering facial expressions, and I can tell he's trying to hold it all in.

"I'm just tired, Yo, I'm tired of fighting, I'm tired of hearing comments, I'm tired of just not knowing if I'll be safe."

He shifts in his seat.

"I just feel like life will be easier if I just turn it down a couple of notches and blend in."

He sniffs and looks away.

"You're not turning notches or flipping switches, Bash, you're being yourself, and if anyone has taught me how important that is, it's you. Screw what people think."

"Yohan, it's not about others' opinions. You're not seeing the bigger picture. For instance, people won't instantly single you out when you walk the streets. You have that shield."

"Sometimes it's not about fighting back; it's about feeling safe, and you, I bet you can go out and not second guess if you might be doing too much for other people's liking. I'm sorry, Yo-Yo, but I don't have that luxury."

I see the tears being held back, his eyes glossy, but I know him. He's too strong to let one fall, not because he wants to be strong, but because he feels like he has to be.

I feel my heart sink because I know he's right; I don't know how he feels, and I don't even know that if we weren't both pretending to be people, we weren't when we first met if we would even be friends right now.

"I'm sorry, Bash."

"It's not your fault." He says now, avoiding all eye contact with the camera.

W-What happened? I ask, trying to carefully navigate the situation because I can tell that he is extremely vulnerable right now, and I am not used to this side of him.

"It's pointless to relive it, really. I think I need some fresh air. Going to head out and take a walk. I'll talk to you later."

Before I can find the right words to reply, the chat screen closes, and the little green bubble that was once filled with life dies to a dull gray.

I can't help but play out scenes in my head about what could've happened to Bash. I don't think it was physical, thank God, because he didn't seem to have any marks or bruises. Maybe they just built up over time, the comments, the emotions...

I know people aren't too welcoming of the idea of a guy wearing makeup, but who really cares? He isn't hurting anybody. I just hope he can bounce back from this. Honestly, I love his creative expression; it makes him, him. A sort of transformation from Sebastian to Bash, the side of him he really identifies with, and I prefer to see him happy.

I try not to think too hard about Bash, and just hope he is ok. I need to get ready for work, so I take a quick shower and get dressed for the day. As I am throwing on my work shirt, I hear a ping from across the room.

Where the hell is my damn phone?

I sort through the mess on my bed of colored pencils, unfinished sketches, and candy wrappers to find my phone under my pillow, indicator light flashing.

I unlock my phone to reveal a new text.

Hey, don't forget your ID tag. They really hate that. I forgot mine on my second day and never heard the end of it, lol.

Crap. I totally would've forgotten—Stoner brain.

Got it! Thanks. Bakery after work, right?

Yes, they have amazing Sushi Pie rolls.

Sushi Pie rolls?

Omg. You have no idea, you'll see.

I exit out of the text thread and slide my phone into my back pocket. It's almost time to head out since I'm deciding to walk today. I think Bash had the right idea about clearing the mind with a walk through nature, so I'm jumping on board.

Before I head out of our apartment, I decide to stop in the kitchen and grab one of my dad's empanadas. He is fantastic at making them; I don't know how, but they always turn out perfect, and to say I have the munchies right now would be putting it lightly.

"See ya later, Pops," I yell as I make my way out of the door and down the stairs of our building.

When I get outside, I am immediately stunned by the brightness of the light coming from the sun since our apartment has darker tones, and to be honest, my emotions are more aligned with my apartment setting than the energy outside is giving right now, but I adjust.

I bite into my empanada, and the flavors are comforting, temporarily elevating my mood as I chew away at its buttery, flaky goodness, but before I know it, I've devoured the whole thing, and my mind goes back to my endless thoughts.

I try to distract myself by taking in the scenery as I make my way to work. The leaves are beautiful, and I can't help but kick a few for fun as I make my way through the streets of Wellwash Springs.

I see the occasional families walking together, laughing, probably sharing memories, and it brings back my own memories of my mom and how close we were when I was a child. I still talk to her occasionally, but it's nothing like it used to be, not that I remember too much of it. I was young.

Would my life be different if I had stayed with her? She never left Shipton. Maybe if I stayed in one city, I could've built something substantial for my life.

I don't know; I believe in fate, and in all the research I've done trying to figure out the meaning of life, *they* say you can't really escape what's meant for you. Who are *they*? I haven't quite figured out that part yet, but whoever *they* are, they have a lot to say.

Wellwash Springs is everything described in every book I've ever read about anything magical and believe me. I've read most of them in search of something to take my life from dull to full of color and vibrancy.

The creepy vibes are here, the constant wonder, and just the feeling that something crazy could happen at any moment.

Or maybe that's just my mind.

Either way, I dig it. I know I just got here, but out of all the places I've been to recently, this one fits my personality the most, it keeps me calm, and I hope we stay this time.

Actually, I hope I stay.

My dad is right. It's time for me to get going, and I wouldn't mind building a foundation here.

My thoughts are skipping at random, from not wanting to disappoint my dad to trying not to worry about Bash, to wondering about my mom, and finally landing on what might be really triggering these emotions piling on right now.

My own issues with identity and what's going on with me.

As I continue my walk to work, I do the math.

I'm in a new place, which means I'll meet new people, which equals waiting to see if I will be accepted or rejected.

I'm all too familiar with these feelings. It's been three years and three different cities, and for some reason, I'm always nervous and always anxious about revealing my truths. I want people to know who I am, but I also want them to accept me.

But which one is more important? Or are they equally important? Does one outweigh the other?

Aella and Lexie seem cool from the little bits and pieces I've gathered about them so far, but it's only been one day. I'm hoping we'll be all right after dinner or lunch or whatever you call a bakery meetup.

I really hope so.

I make the last turn on the street leading to my job, and I can see the big bright letters illuminated on the building: FURNISH.

I try extremely hard to clear my head as I approach the building, putting in as much effort as possible to wipe away any negative thoughts.

As I press my badge to the scanner, I have one last thought funneling through my already crowded mind.

You'll let them know at dinner, Yohan. It'll be fine.

Lexie

"**A** FRIGGING WITCH! ELLA, I'm telling you, Yohan is a witch!"

I look over at a customer with a desk organizer in her hand. Her eyes are wide open, and her mouth agape, so it's more than obvious she is listening in on Aella and I's conversation... subtlety is clearly not her forte.

Ella places her hand on my shoulder.

"Yeah, Lex, that IS a crazy plot twist in that movic you guys watched last night. Xyla must have loved it," Aella says, forcing a giggle.

I lower my voice. "Great save." I chuckle and turn my back so the customer stops staring intrusively.

"But seriously, though, he's a freaking witch. I got this weird email last night when I was applying for jobs, and before you ask, no, I am not opening random links. I thought it was a reply to one of my applications."

"Okay, but what does this have to do with Yohan?"

"If you would let me finish...."

"Anyway, there was a part of the email that had this image, something called Aiden's spiral. I think it was, yeah, Aiden's spiral and that symbol under it. It was the same as one of Yohan's tattoos."

Ella places her hand over her mouth like this is some breaking news on YNN.

"Oh my God, slash Goddess! ... I like to keep an open mind."

"I know, right?"

I fidget around at the desk we're standing at to give off the impression that we are hard at work just in case management strolls by because I know I'm already on their *people we can afford to get rid of* list.

"Well, did you ask him? I mean, you have his number, right? If not, I do, and we can solve this right now."

She whips out her phone, unlocks it, and begins to type.

"NO! Don't." I place my hand quickly over her phone.

"I did text him, but not about that. I sent him a *reminder* text about his ID tag, hoping it would guilt him into a confession once he saw how nice I was."

"Okay, and?" she replies, as she's now joining me in randomly moving things around to help upsell the illusion of two hard-at-work employees.

"It didn't work. He's all like *ok*, and like *bakery later* blah, blah, blah."

"Oh yeah, Eat Your Heart Out Bakery, the perfect time to ask him! And I'll be there for support. He can't avoid it then."

"Avoid what?"

I hear a calm, carefree voice behind me, and I instantly know it's Yo-Yo.

Oh shit.

I turn around to quickly to face him.

"Can't avoid...."

I frantically look around, trying to come up with a fast response.

"Can't avoid... doing work, newbie. Yesterday was your easy day, but not today. Today, you shall work."

"Yes, it's been decided!" Aella chimes in.

He chuckles.

"Yeah, I mean.... I kind of expected that, seeing as how I am at... Work."

He raises an eyebrow.

"Yea, ha-ha," I giggle.

Sarcastic, secretive, little bitch, I'm on to you.

I notice Ella is staring at his tattoo, like seriously?

Could she make it any more obvious?

Hoping to clear the now awkward air occupying the space between the three of us, I think of a quick diversion because I cannot have this conversation here, especially not with these customers/eavesdroppers.

"First task of the day, Yohan, sign into the learning computer and get those trainings done. The quicker you do, the faster we get you out here on the sales floor, and then the real fun begins."

"What fun?" Aella chimes in once again.

"Omg, shut up, Ella." I roll my eyes.

They both laugh as if my being irritated is comical.

I direct both him and Ella towards our training desk, located to the side of our department, behind a translucent divider, and ask her to get him signed in.

I'm trusting that she can avoid the topic of his tattoo, along with my many suspicions, while she gets him all set up to do his mandatory courses.

As I make my way back to my station, I pull out my compact, do a quick hair and makeup check, and go back to looking busy, now organizing all the little accessories we have for offices.

The cute little organizers, the mouse pads, the clicky pens, and, of course, the customizable laptop stands.

Oh, I could totally use one of these. Yes, this, too! This is EVERY-THING!

My mental shopping list is just getting longer and longer.

I intend on doing some actual work today, but in the back of my mind, I can't help but run several scenarios about why Yohan would send me that email and why he would target... me.

How did he even get my email address? Did he run a reverse search on one of those sketchy websites with my phone number? Was my contact information forwarded to him when we exchanged numbers?

OH. MY. GOD. Did he stalk my social media?

"What if he, like, stalked your social media?"

I jump and notice Ella behind me with a quizzical look on her face.

"Girl, get out of my head. I was just thinking that, well, whatever the case may be, we'll figure it out tonight. This day needs to hurry up and be over with already because I have tons of questions."

"Tons." Ella agrees.

We look over at Yohan, who is currently spaced out at the computer screen. It's kind of funny how hard he seems to be concentrating on the tutorial because I'm pretty sure I randomly selected answers at every quiz intertwined within those dreaded staff training sessions.

Honestly, I wanted to award myself a medal or two for staying awake through those damn things.

Ella leans back on the desk behind us, and I follow suit. She's fidgeting with the tie I got for her back on her sixteenth birthday, the one with the blood spatters.

I got it because of her ongoing vampire obsession, and I think it complements her red hair perfectly.

I notice she's staring at him, but hell, so am I. I hope he doesn't look over and notice.

Please don't notice.

Ella redirects her attention to me.

"You've got to admit. He's a cute witch, though."

She bites her bottom lip.

"Yeah, I've noticed, though I had to wait until I got into work yesterday to see for myself because you refused to give me details via text."

I send an unmistakable look of annoyance her way.

"But we need to put the cute part aside for now." "We absolutely need to figure this guy out," I say, all while secretly in a daze of my own.

"Right, anyway, this day won't go any faster by us sitting here and daydreaming, I'll handle customers, and you got the merch?" she asks gleefully.

I'll never understand why she'd choose customer interaction.

"I wouldn't have it any other way," I respond, overcome with a sense of relief.

I tried my best to stick to working on processing paperwork, stocking merchandise, and checking on Yohan in between tasks, just to make sure he hadn't died of boredom or something from the countless videos and quizzes he's been subjected to for the day. Still, it was almost impossible to avoid the customers.

Just as I refer to my job as the *Torture Chamber,* the customers are definitely the self-proclaimed masochists who keep the joint running.

First, there was the lady who cussed me out because, apparently, she drove two hours to get these lime green binders that weren't currently in stock, and, oh yeah, our website begged to differ.

I guess taking five minutes to order them online just wasn't an option for her. She'd rather spend twenty minutes insisting on the fact that it was my fault.

Then, of course, who could forget the guy who told me, "If *The Creator* wanted my hair pink, He would've made it that way."?

I wanted to say, "Well, *They* created the person who created this fabulous pink weave, so..." but instead, I smiled, and he proceeded to push a pamphlet toward me.

And lastly, the thirst buckets.

The men who most likely have loyal girlfriends or wives at home insist on saying things like, "I'll totally buy this if you promise you'll be the one to come over and put it together."

Or my favorite, "What is a girl as beautiful as you doing working at a store like this?"

Trying to make some money, dipshit. Go back home to Becky.

Thank God for Jaden, the coworker who is always looking to brown nose his way to the top.

He noticed my frustration during several of my customer interactions throughout the day and stepped in like the champ he is, saving me from possibly reacting irrationally and losing my job.

Oh, cookie dough whiskey, how I miss you so. I need a shot after this. Maybe two.

It's finally time to head out of here, and it's definitely not one of those cases where it's *before I know it.*

In actuality, the day dragged on like hell, but somehow, it managed to move along, and the workday thankfully passed by.

We leave the dreary doors of FURNISH and head towards Eat Your Heart Out Bakery.

Finally, the chance of a peaceful night becomes more realistic.

Hmph, yeah, right, peace?

You are about to let this guy know you know his secret.

It's. About. To. Go. Down.

I sigh.

"What's wrong? We've escaped!" Ella says, now skipping, her tie dancing in the wind.

"Yeah, at least your eyes aren't torn to shreds from staring at a computer screen all day. Every time I blink, I feel like there are little glass shards under my eyelids."

I notice his exaggerated display, blinking repetitively and squinting his eyes like a baby when they first sense bright light.

I can't help but laugh.

"As if we're not in the digital age, I want to see you avoid staring at a screen for just one day, and we'll see how far you get."

"She's got a point," says Ella, now slowing down to walk and meet our pace.

"Eh, I guess," Yohan responds.

As we continue our walk, we swap stories about our day at FUR-NISH, mainly Ella and I, with the addition of what seems like occasional forced comments from Yohan here and there.

I mean, I can't blame him. What he did at work today could've basically been accomplished from home, which, in my opinion, the company should totally allow.

I'm getting antsy even though I know we will be approaching the bakery soon enough, but I can't help but think of how to tackle this upcoming conversation.

I know I have Ella as backup, and she's an excellent partner in crime, but I don't want to appear abrasive... what if all this is just a coincidence?

Highly unlikely, Lexie, but what if?

Either way, it has to be done.

As we finally make it to the entranceway of Eat Your Heart Out Bakery, I can see the shocked look on Yohan's face, and I can tell this is not at all what he was expecting.

"Welcome to the coolest place in Wellwash Springs, Yo-Yo. I now present to you *Eat Your Heart Out Bakery,*" says Ella performatively with a spin ending in open arms at the bakery's doors.

Dramatic much?

I can't help but serve up one of my signature eye-rolls, paired with a giggle.

We make our way in, and that glossy look of awe is still emanating from Yohan's face. I'm starting to wonder if it may now be painted on permanently.

Aella and I can't seem to help but respond by exchanging nudges and low chuckles at his sense of intrigue as we're walking, heading toward our favorite table.

Yes, we are regulars.

I can see she is just as amused as I am by Yohan's bewildered looks of amazement as he takes the place in, eyes darting from wall to wall, smirking, gesturing toward me and Ella from time to time.

"This is insane. Absolutely insane."

His reactions are reminiscent of my first time here as well, although I am surprised that someone with such a bad-boy, punk rock style didn't discover this place himself first thing after his move.

"I know, right?" Me and Ella say in unison.

The thing about Eat Your Heart Out Bakery is that it's not a bakery at all.

The story goes: The owners named it that to suggest that you come here when you are entirely "baked" to get the full effect of its eccentric flare.

It's more of a restaurant/bar meets hookah spot with a lovable eerie twist.

The place honestly pays homage to vampires and creatures of the night, and yes, Aella found it first. The girl just loves the idea of a bloodthirsty hottie.

From the dark color scheme to the smoky-filled ambiance, this place would basically make the gothy folks go bat-shit, for lack of a better term.

"This is sick. Freaking sick."

"Okay, Yohan, you've already said that."

"Yeah, now you're just switching verbiage... we get it, you love it!" says Ella, pulling up a chair at our favorite table and displaying a huge smile.

Ella loves introducing people to new things and feels extremely accomplished when they like them.

In all honesty, she has shown me many cool things here and there throughout our friendship, and it really makes me appreciate her even more.

We're settling in, and I notice Ella staring at me intensely.

If you think I'm just going to go ahead and blurt out an accusation here, you don't know me well. This must be handled delicately, then, boom, pounce, attack.

My thought process is interrupted by Yohan's question.

"So, what's good here? What about those sushi pie rolls you suggested?"

"Oh my gosh, Lexie, those are supposed to be a surprise for first-timers! They are unique and deserve respect."

She points a finger at me, wagging it repeatedly. I guess I'm being scolded.

"Oh, I wasn't informed," I say, trying not to sound sarcastic.

"Well, I'm starting with a drink, the Blood Bath. It's strong and will erase the thoughts of FURNISH from my mind, for today at least."

"Oh my God, yes, ditto." Ella quickly agrees.

I notice Yohan perusing the menu, trying to figure it all out, reading the descriptions underneath the little vampire-inspired code names for the drinks.

We probably should have been offering suggestions, saying what's good and what to stay away from, but in all actuality, I've enjoyed everything I've tried here so far, and to be honest, there are bigger fish to fry.

He finally peers up from the menu, still looking as unsure as when he started.

"I guess make it three." He finally says, probably not wanting to keep us waiting.

There's time, anyway.

Time for drinks, time for food, time for bonding.

But most of all...

The time for confrontation, there's definitely time for confrontation.

A waitress who seems to be around our age wearing a name badge displaying "Patra" comes and takes our order.

She seems nice, just a tad bit off. I can't really describe it. Maybe her personality is supposed to fit in with the vampire theme; I can't tell, and I really don't care. I just want my drink.

Once she leaves, the table quickly grows a bit tense, all of us staring at our phones, occasionally looking at one another without saying a word.

"So, you guys come here a lot?" says Yohan, forcing conversation to kill the silence.

"Yeah, we've been coming here for a while now, actually like two years, ever since we turned twenty-one," replies Ella.

She continues rambling, letting Yohan know how she discovered Eat Your Heart Out Bakery. She then goes into her theory about vampires and how they do exist before our waitress eventually cuts her off.

Patra arrives with our three Bloodbaths and sets the drinks before us individually.

The drinks are crimson red and fashioned with dry ice that form cute little smoke clouds now hovering over the rims of our cocktail glasses.

"Enjoy," she says eerily, showing her teeth in what I think is an attempt at a smile as she walks away sheepishly.

I take a sip of my drink and feel that warm feeling in my chest, the one that motivates me to get up and get going, delivering me that much-needed kick.

"Hmm, this tastes interesting. What is this pomegranate, right?"

There he goes, trying again to force conversation. Let it happen naturally, guy. You are trying too hard.

I notice Ella blankly staring at me again from the corner of my eye. It's becoming too much.

God, I can't take another minute of this.

Not another minute.

Go time.

I spit it out.

"So nice tattoos, Yohan. I particularly like the one on your forearm, Aiden's Spiral, right?"

There, I did it. I said it.

He looks stunned, or maybe puzzled, but not startled, not startled at all. He looks...

Curious.

Just as curious as me, like he wants to know more....

After what seems like forever, he answers me......calmly.

No wait.

It's not an answer.

It's a question.

"How do you know about Aiden's Spiral?"

Chapter Four

Aella

G OTCHA BY YOUR STRING, *Mr. Yo-Yo. Not so tough now, huh?*

Ha-ha, I made a pun.

Lexie's terracotta skin tone looks absolutely stunning in this dim light.

Wait, what am I doing? There's a confession about to happen.

I shift my focus back to the table.

"Ok, so what is this Aiden's Spiral thing you guys keep talking about? It's all out in the open now. Come on, Yo-Yo, spit it out. You have the symbol tattooed on your body, for goodness' sake, so it must mean something to you."

I feel so relieved to get that off my chest. The thoughts about this email have been circulating in my mind all day. I wanted to confront him myself, but since Lexie was the one who received the message, I knew I better leave it to her.

"Screw the spiral."

Lexie slams her hand down on the table.

Wasn't expecting that...

"Why are you sending me weird, cryptic emails?"

"And how did you even get my email address to begin with?"

"Yeah," I chime in.

"Okay, first off, I don't even know what email you are talking about, and second, I just met you yesterday. We exchanged numbers, and that's it. I don't have your email address."

He seems to be getting a little agitated, but I mean, Lexie did throw an accusation out there, but that's the way you have to do it, no B.S, straight to the point, catch the culprit when they least expect it, that's the only way to get the truth.

"Yeah, I bet, so I meet you one day, then go home, and suddenly, I get an email with an attachment that just so happens to have an image of the same symbol you have tattooed permanently on your skin?"

"Doesn't seem to be a coincidence to me. What do you think, Ella?"

I sip my drink. My eyes widen, and I shake my head from side to side.

"Nope, doesn't seem like a coincidence."

"Well, where is this so-called email you are referencing? Seems like all accusations and no evidence."

I can tell he is trying to keep calm, which in my mind comes off as a bit suspicious, but his overall mannerisms are a bit strange, to begin with, so I have no idea what angle this guy is playing.

"I deleted it. I thought it might've been a virus, but then I remembered where I saw the symbol..."

"On your freaking arm!"

"Of course, you deleted it," he responds, rolling his eyes.

Hey, that's Lexie's move, new guy. Watch your facial expressions!

"Well, did you empty your trash after?"

Lexie pauses.

"As a matter of fact, no, I didn't! Aha!"

She pulls out her phone, and I'm getting even more excited as I wait for her to navigate to her email. I want to see this in person to see if it is as thought-provoking as she described it to be.

I can't wait. I'm at the edge of my seat, sipping the last bits of my cocktail, waiting for the big reveal.

She plops her phone on the table so it's in view, and we move in closer to get a good look.

She doesn't even have to scroll. The first thing on the attachment to the email is the text displaying Aiden's *Spiral.*

Aidens Spiral
Used for protection, symbolizes protection by fire.
Can protect an individual from advanced forms of magic.
Use with caution.
Due to Aiden's Spiral's association with fire, its projection is known to cause adverse heat-related effects, permanent delusion, and, in extreme cases, DEATH.
Use is only intended for the pure of heart.
Only those whose intentions come from a place of innocence may obtain and use this ability.

Summoning Aiden's Spiral
Aiden's spiral requires advanced visualization. See in the mind's eye the jagged spiral, focus on the center, will it to spin, as it spins, envision the spiral beginning to light at its end, project...

"Ok, I'm sorry, this looks like a bunch of bullshit to me, like some roleplaying crap, definitely spam."

"Omg, that's what I thought, until well, Yohan over there and his ...body art. Any comments, sir? Feel free to join in on this conversation at any point."

He looks up from the phone screen and seems to be taking this much more seriously than we are. There's a look of fear in his eyes or amazement. I can't really tell. Once again, this guy's personality throws me off completely.

"I can't believe what I'm seeing. I've heard about this but sometimes questioned if it was real. I thought it might've been some guy messing around on the internet, like a message board troll or something."

He attempts to keep reading the attachment on Lexie's phone, but she snatches it up almost as quickly as he peers his eyes back down.

"Who? What guy? Yohan, what are you talking about?!"

I can tell she's growing impatient, and to be honest, so am I. I feel like for a confrontation, we've gotten absolutely nowhere.

He continues.

"So, I've always kind of been into the metaphysical, you know, researching different belief systems, trying to find out the truth about life and whatnot."

"Uh-huh," Lexie says dryly.

"Long story short."

A little too late for that, buddy.

"I was on a message board for, you know, occult type things, séances, spells, meditations, you know, just for people interested in finding out if magic was real..."

"I ran into a guy who called himself Zeus. He mentioned something called the Book of Ascension. He said it was the key to ensure that in the life after this one, an individual would transcend into something greater, that they would basically become a powerhouse in the next life, and that's the main reason for the book's existence, to grant an upper hand in this lifetime which in turn determines your status in the next."

"He said I would eventually find what I was looking for, you know… answers.

"He showed me the symbol, Aiden's Spiral, and said it was mentioned in the book and that it was the highest symbol of protection against harmful magic and ill intent."

"He never told me how to use it or why, and honestly, I don't know why I believed him, but I just kind of intuitively felt it might be true, like an inclination that what he was saying was rooted in absolute fact."

I give him the most incredible look of confusion I can muster up because what he is saying sounds so farfetched, so made up, and I cannot believe what I am hearing.

"So, you believe this?" I say, raising my eyebrow.

"I believe anything is possible, and seeing as how Lexie over here got this email out of nowhere, it has to mean something."

Lexie chimes in.

"Okay, whatever, let's say this Book of Ascension is real, and I somehow now have the key to afterlife domination. That still doesn't explain why the symbol is tattooed on your damn body! Like, can we focus here?"

The girls got a point.

"I got the tattoo because after talking to Zeus, I couldn't find anything or anyone else who knew about this mysterious book, but what I COULD find was information on Aiden's Spiral, a sort of leak, I guess."

Did Lexie not research any of this? If Yo-Yo could find something online about Aiden's Spiral, I'm sure she could have.

"Well, what did you find?" I ask, trying to use a neutral tone.

"It wasn't easy. Regular search engines brought up nothing, but I had a friend named Max back in Tollsbrook who was a total techy, so I told him about Aiden's Spiral, and he ran a search on the dark web. Apparently, there's a subculture of witches there that exchange information."

Lexie looks from Yohan to me; her face seems concerned, and I can already tell what she's thinking. She doesn't even have to say it.

This guy is crazy as hell.

I chuckle in my head and continue to listen to Yohan's explanation.

"I have this tattoo because I believe there are things out there, things out there that are truly evil, and my friend found out that this symbol, Aiden's Spiral, is like ultimate protection."

"Now, I know you might think this is all a bit crazy, but if there is something out there, I rather ward it off with a bit of body art than be completely defenseless."

"But I mean, why would they be targeting you? These so-called High Ascension wizard people? Are you a witch, too? Have you been performing these rituals and crap you found on your message board rampages?"

I notice Lexie chuckling to herself. She's no longer taking any of this seriously, and to be honest, it is kind of funny how he is so invested in this online magical conspiracy theory.

"I've tried a thing or two, but nothing ever happened. I think the stuff that the public can access isn't the real deal. Now, the stuff Max found, the stuff on the dark web, I think it's legit."

Lexie slides her phone back into her front shirt pocket.

"Okay, Yohan, you're cool and all, but you are officially on my list of crazies, ha-ha, cool but a little nutzo."

He laughs it off. I don't think he's offended at all. I mean, anyone in their right mind would expect people hearing a story like that to be skeptical, hell I would be, and I sure am.

"I think we need shots! A round of Scythe Wielders?" Lexie suggests.

Perfect timing.

"OMG, yes, and yes, you are going to love these Yo-Yo!"

Our waitress, Patra, returns to our table, and we get our shots and order a mini sushi pie platter. I love the pumpkin pie rolls. They are amazing, especially in the autumn. They just give me all the vibes.

"So, I think I've had enough supernatural talk for one day. How was your day minus the brain-draining session FURNISH gifted you today?"

I'm still stuffing my face with rolls, so I'm basically a spectator at this point.

Strawberry cheesecake rolls, I've determined your fate. Into my belly, you go...

"My day was... long..."

I manage to stop chewing for a second to ask, "Why, what happened?"

"Just my dad, you know, complaining about me getting my shit together, the usual parental crap."

"Tell me about it. I've grown to expect the daily lectures my parents serve constantly," Lexie responds, of course, with an eye roll.

"Yeah, and I'm kind of worried about my buddy Bash. He wasn't in the greatest mood the last time I talked to him, and you know he's just not like that. I've never seen the guy not try to find the bright side in any situation."

"Well, everyone gets a little shaken up by life occasionally. I'm sure he'll be ok."

"Yeah." I chime in, "The rough times make you stronger. I know it's cliché, but totally true."

"...and I know this might also sound like one of those things you say in the moment, but me and Lex are totally here if you need to talk. We're a team now, the tortured of FURNISH."

Lexie bursts out into a laugh. "Totally the tortured of FURNISH."

I notice Yohan giving a little laugh that's completely inauthentic, and he starts looking down at the table, using his sugar-molded chopsticks to move one of his Crème Brûlée pie rolls back and forth.

"You alright, Yohan? Are the drinks kicking in? Because I get it, I feel the buzz, too. I'm a total lightweight now, Lex. She's the drinker."

"Yeah, paint me out to be an alcoholic, Ella. That's what we wanna do on our first outing with Mr. Yo-Yo here."

She tosses a crumpled-up napkin at me; I catch it and stick my tongue out teasingly.

"Actually, there's something I need to tell you guys."

Omg, he totally sent the email, and he's feeling guilty.

His head is still down, and I see Lexie look over at me, and I'm again sure I know her thoughts align with mine.

Yep, he sent it. Here comes the confession we've been waiting for all day.

"All ears," I say.

"Yeah, after the conversation we just had, I doubt anything else can be shocking, really." She adds.

"I'm gay."

Lies. Lexie. Lies... This is definitely shocking.

"It's totally cool if you guys don't want to talk to me anymore. I'm used to it. I've moved around so much, and I always get mixed responses. I figured I'd just throw it out there. I mean, I like you guys, and I get it if it's too much, just after everything with Bash and the makeup, and I don't know I…"

Lexie interjects.

"Yohan, first off, you are rambling, Hun, and second, we wouldn't have invited you to our favorite spot if we didn't already like you, gay, straight … potential master of Aiden's Spiral, you are accepted all the same."

I watch as she scoots closer to him to hug him and notice he's got a tear coming down.

This guy can't be out to get us. What were we thinking? I mean, in the case that I might be wrong, this is quite the diversion he is setting up, and he is a freaking mastermind.

"I'm just happy you're not a serial killer," I respond, as I gesture a heart symbol toward him, which makes him roll into laughter.

"Ha. I guess that's fair. If I were on the other end of this mess, I would probably think the same."

"Would you guys like anything else? Another round of shots, maybe?"

I didn't even notice our waitress standing there. She moves so covertly it's creepy.

I look from Yohan to Lex. "Calling it a night, you guys? I think I should probably catch a ride with my brothers while I can. Those guys are always all over the place. The only good thing is I get to have the apartment all to myself most of the time."

"Right. I should probably head out, too. Xyla's probably got a mouthful of stories from playing detective all afternoon that she's dying to share with me."

"I think we'll take the check," Lexie replies to Patra, who then grabs some of our empty dining ware, stacks it on a tray, and proceeds to the kitchen.

We gather our things and head out of the bakery laughing and now having an actual conversation, which seems less forced than the attempt we tried earlier on the walk here.

Yohan tells us bits and pieces about moving from place to place and about some of the people he's met.

He's actually a cool guy and an artist. I can't wait to see some of his pieces, even though, by the descriptions, they seem strange, but art is art, nonetheless.

They are both amicable enough to keep me company while I wait for my brothers to pick me up. These guys are always late.

I offered both Yo and Lex rides home. Not like I'm the one driving, but hey, what's the use of being a triplet if you can't call in favors?

They both decline, Lexie, wanting to catch a Dryve because she has a stop she wants to make before going home. I'm almost sure it's to restock her cookie dough whiskey.

Yohan said he wanted to take a walk, enjoy the scenery, maybe take an alternate route, and explore his new home, Wellwash Springs.

I told him there wasn't much to see, but hey, his choice.

I see my brothers' car in the near distance, so I get ready to make my way towards the sidewalk so I'm easy for them to spot.

"Bye, guys!" I give them hugs and promise to shoot a text later to make sure everyone has gotten home safely.

As I enter the car, I greet my brothers.

"Hey Aeden, Hey Aesher, thanks for the ride."

"Who's the guy?" Aedan asks.

"Yeah, who's the guy? Is that Lexie's new boyfriend or something?"

"He's our new coworker, Aesher..."

"Get a grip. Aren't you over your crush already? Lexie's so not into you." I tell him for the umpteenth time.

"Yeah, she's into me. She thinks I'm the hot one, bro, I can tell."

"We're identical asshole."

I tune them out as the car makes its way to our apartment, and I'm replaying the day in my head...

The long day at work.

The drinks at the bakery.

Yohan, trusting us enough to come out.

That crazy email.

Ha-Ha Aiden's Spiral, project the spiral, see it spin.

Spin for me, bitch! Spin!

Ha-Ha

What a crock of shit.

Heat-related effects... who comes up with this crap?

Warning may cause delusion or death. Ha-Ha.

Wait...

What the eff?

DEATH?!

Didn't Yohan say he couldn't find much about the spiral besides what Max dug up on the dark web?

Death?

Oh. My. GOD.

Did Yohan mistakenly mark himself for death?

CHAPTER FIVE

Aella

*N*O, HE CAN'T DIE.

He just can't.

I know I just met him, but I like the guy, or at least what I know of him so far.

"Bye, Ella, we'll be back, and don't touch my leftover drunken noodles. I have plans for those!" Aesher yells as their car pulls off.

As I make my way into our apartment, I'm considering going online to do some research for myself on this whole ordeal, but then I remember what Yohan said about the lack of knowledge being available to the public, and I sure as hell don't want to go digging around on the dark web.

Instead, I make my way to my room and turn on some music to decompress from the day. I need to have a moment of peace with all this new information buzzing around in my mind.

I grab my tablet, open my design app, and start to scroll through the tie designs I've drafted so far.

Starting a collection is more challenging than I thought. I'm running out of ideas, and if I'm going to stick out, I'll need something creative to catch the eye of the bigwigs.

Something as unique as the tie Lexie got for me.

I look down at the tie, still dangling from my neck in all its glory, with all the detail, all the strategically placed blood splatters. It's so vampire chic.

This is why she's my ride-or-die. She totally gets me...

I scroll through my collection, which is still under construction, and can't help but slip into a fantasy of the runway.

My runway.

I can see it all so clearly...

"Now debuting a new line of ties for all occasions, stunning and sophisticated, both elegant and bold, we bring you the Trinity collection from upcoming designer Aella Callahan."

Ah, that would be so kick ass.

I snap back to reality and keep scrolling.

The one with safety pins is my favorite idea I've come up with so far. It's kind of edgy but can still be pulled off in a formal setting, at least in my opinion.

I need something that really makes a statement, something whimsical but fashion-forward, eye-catching but cute...

Think, Ella, think.

A notification pops up on my tablet.

Daily Affirmation: Thank you, universe, for showing me the answers to every problem.

I can't help but giggle.

Well, Mr. or Mrs. Universe, can you help me think of a unique tie design for my collection?

Oh yeah, and by the way, is my new friend going to die? Can you show me the answer to that problem?

I swipe the notification away, roll my eyes, and chuckle to myself.

I pause and look up from the screen of my tablet to think for a second.

...wait, maybe you can.

...the cards can.

I can't help but get a little antsy in my seat because I finally have a legitimate reason to feed my ongoing tarot addiction.

It definitely beats my usual questions like:

Does the guy in the apartment on the floor above me really like me?

Will I get a new job by the end of the year?

And the number one resounding question,

Will I ever get a place of my own?

I could do the reading myself because I have my own sets of cards, but I like to watch readings online from time to time to peek in on other readers' insights.

I haven't really read for anyone other than myself. It's more of a hobby and a kind of secret hobby at that.

No one really knows, not even my brothers, unless they've been sneaking around in my room, and I wouldn't put it past them.

Nosey little bastards.

I close out my design app and fight the urge to just let these thoughts go. I have to at least try to get a better understanding of this situation. What if, for some reason, all of this is real, and we somehow have opened Pandora's box?

Or, in this case, Aiden's.

Okay, this is not the most logical way to go about this, but are we really dealing with logic anymore?

No. We're dealing with witchcraft and mysticism, so I think this is warranted.

I open my web browser and navigate to MeView.

Come on, sketchy online tarot readers, you must have something for me.

I type in Gemini Tarot readings and click on the first one I see that's dated for this month's predictions.

The reader pops up on the screen and starts shuffling the cards immediately, welcoming me to her MeView page and asking me to subscribe and like her channel.

I sit through the drawn-out intro, and her reading finally begins.

"Hey, my lovely Geminis, oh man, it looks like it will be a rough month for you guys."

She starts to lay the cards out on the table.

"To start, we have the Tower. It looks like things are shaking up a bit here, followed by the death card, and oh geez, next, we have the three of swords."

"Hold on tight, my Gems, because it looks like…"

I pause the video.

No way, the death card?

Okay, let's try another one. There are a million of these; they can't all say the same thing, and it's loose guidance at best. Besides, the stuff made public isn't real, right?

I scroll past about ten MeView videos of Gemini monthly predictions and click on the one that says, "Great News Gemini."

This one can't be bad. It literally says, "Great News".

I click on the video, and it begins to play.

The tarot reader seems a bit young. His background is bright blue with crystals lined all along the walls behind him, his blond hair dangling before his face as he shuffles his cards, smiling at the camera.

Okay, now this is more like it. Come on CrystalMage, what cha got for me?

"Hey, my Gemini's, welcome back, and thank you for joining me once again,"

"Remember, if you like my style and are picking up on my vibe, don't forget to click that bell to subscribe and like my video."

Yeah, I know, I know, come on, get to it, love.

He starts shuffling the cards, his eyes straying away from the camera now and then as he lays them down on the table.

"All right, Gems. So the good news is that change is coming in, and it's coming in fast."

He points the camera down at the table so it's now in view, and I cannot believe what I am seeing.

"Looks like you have a tower moment coming. Not to fear, though, even though these moments might feel a little tough to get through. Once you are through my Gem, things only go up from there."

Screw the tower. Screw the other cards. Get to the death card already!

"Now I know you're probably getting a little worried because you see the death card here in the spread."

You think?

"But death does not mean literal death; it means something is ending, and with the tower card here, I can see that overall, you are transforming, my dear Gemini and it's nothing to fear. Transformation can be beautiful."

Yeah, tell that to a mutant...

"The best advice I can give is just to stay strong and push through, even though there may be some heartbreak..."

I stop the video as he holds the three swords to the camera.

Two separate readings, the same core cards...

And death in both?...

Okay, this can't be an accident. I need to reach out because whatever we have gotten ourselves into at this point, I think it's about to get worse.

I reach for my phone and create a group text with Lex and Yohan.

Hey, loves, just checking in to make sure everyone got home safe.

As I wait a few minutes for a response, I close out MeView and toss my tablet to the side.

Hey, yeah, I'm home. The bakery was awesome. We definitely should go back soon. Btw, I really appreciate you guys being there for me today. I really needed it.

Of course, remember we are the tortured of TURNISH. It's a thing now. Lol

Hey, I'm home, lol. What's with the title of the grouper? Ha-ha, Haus of Ascension? Love it. *cry laugh emoji*

Omg, I didn't even notice that. I second that. Love it! *heart*

I mean, we're all stunning, so you know, I thought I'd add a bit of flare to our text train.

Lexie

Yass Queen. We're lit. *kiss*

Yohan

Ha-ha, totally *cool emoji*

So, not to put a damper on things, but…

Lexie

As If we haven't had enough drama for one night, girl, what have you gone and done now?

Yohan

eyes emoji

It's about your tattoo, Yohan. I mean, I don't want to scare you or anything. I could just be overthinking it, but when I came home, I couldn't help but get lost in thought about it.

Yohan

About what? I told you all I know…

Lexie

Yeah, I thought we were past this… Ella girl, I think you just need some sleep.

Girl, I know what it says. I have it in my inbox.
What's the point?

I put my phone down on my desk for a moment.

I'm getting nervous and second-guessing if this is the right thing to do. Should I bring this all up again? Maybe I should just leave it alone and chalk it all up to it being a strange day all around. Everything will be back to normal tomorrow.

No, Ella, you watch these videos; you know about the cards; you know the universe is trying to clue you in. You would be stupid to ignore such a message, such a clear, distinct message...

I pick my phone back up.

Hello?! Earth to Ella. *alien emoji*

I throw my phone on the bed and cover my mouth.

I can't believe I said that they are going to think I'm nuts now.

I'm afraid to look at their responses. God, I could use one of Lexie's cookie dough shots right now.

Can you virtually send me one girl? Is that a thing?

I muster up the courage to get up from my chair and walk over to my bed to pick my phone back up to see what they have to say about my theory.

It can't be good.

Oh shit.

WTF, I didn't even put that together.

Now I'm nervous af, but nothing has happened so far, so I have to be ok right?

You're fine, Hun. Trust me.

Yeah, it can't be. Max said it was for protection, and I haven't been practicing using it. It's just a tattoo design, like any other.

What am I doing? I can't help myself.

I start to type.

Well, maybe you should start practicing using it.

I don't know you guys. I just have a feeling that things are going to get a little crazy. This can't all be happening for no reason.

We can't be like all those people in the movies who just sit and wait to be confronted and have no plan. We're smarter than that. Let's get ahead of the game.

Okay Ella, it's official, no more drinking for you. LMAO *cry laugh emoji*

Still love ya, though. *heart emoji*

Lex, no offense, but I think she might have a point.

Maybe we should be prepared. Worst-case scenario, we have a funny story to share years down the line, but like I said before, I think this stuff is real.

I knew I liked this guy.

Yes, and yes, I say it's time to get magical bitches. *girly hand emoji* *stars*

Lex, do you mind sharing screenshots of the attachment to the grouper so we can review it?

Good Idea. At least we can study it, sleep on
it, and reconvene.

No problem, give me a sec.

I'm getting even more anxious as I wait for the screenshots to pop
up in the grouper because now there's no going back.

We're in deep.

The attachment pops up. I click it and save it to my phone for later.

Got it, thanks!

Same, thanks, Lex.

No problem, you crazies, Haus of Ascen-
sion/Tortured of FURNISH, whatever the
hell we are, we are in it together now.

Ha-ha bet.

Totally.

Well, you guys, I will catch up with you tomorrow at work. I'm tired. I am going to call
it a night. Love Ya!

Me too, Night Honeys. *kiss emoji*

Night *wave emoji*

I plug my phone into the charger, change into my night clothes, and lay in my bed, and the thoughts start to funnel through my head.

Yohan might be in danger.

I'm maybe now a witch.

I love this little friend group.

Maybe I should give these screenshots a quick look.

I'm getting extremely tired, but I choose to open the screenshots anyway to give them a brief review, even though I can barely keep my eyes open.

Yeah, yeah, Aidens Spiral, I've had enough of that for one day, plus I think that's kind of Yohan's thing.

I scroll to the following screenshot.

Hmm, Simple Wishing Spell? Now, this seems more my speed.

Simple Wishing

Chanting holds power. Simply by chanting wishes with pure intent, one may manifest their desires into reality. All the power you need lies within you.

Oh yeah, Lexie always talks about manifesting and using intention or whatnot.

I can barely keep my eyes open, but I attempt to at least a few more lines of the screenshot before I start to doze in and out of sleep.

I attempt to keep reading.

> Create a clear intention of your desires
> and chant the word that you feel embodies
> every aspect of your desire.
> Once you have chosen your word of power,
> feel the feeling of having received your
> wish already. Know it is here, know it is
> yours, you create your reality. There is
> no such thing as coincidence.

Whoever the author is clearly hasn't had a day like mine...

> Now you have the power to manifest your
> every desire, feel the movement, feel the
> completion. When you feel you are ready,
> say the phrase of sealing: Aya Realaze,
> I-din Aya Releaze!

Ha-ha, I release, I did, I release.

I'm so sleepy.

Well, this looks fairly simple.

I mean, maybe we could wish for protection. That couldn't hurt, right?

Yes! That's it. We'll do the wishing spell. It doesn't seem like that could go wrong.

I mean, I'm not dumb. I won't wish for money or anything. That's when people die, and you get an inheritance and shit like that. I've seen those movies.

I shift my body to make myself more comfortable on the bed because this battle between me and sleep is close to its end.

We'll just wish it all away...

I turn off my phone, toss it to the side of the bed, and close my eyes.

Haus of Ascension...

Tortured of FURNISH...

Stand in line and assemble...

We've got some wishing to do!

ZzZzZ...

CHAPTER SIX

Yohan

"**G**ET OFF OF HER, you bitch!"

Ella motions her hand in a wave, and the creature flies across the room, slamming into the desk in the middle of the showroom.

The customers are visibly panic stricken as they run aimlessly in all directions, attempting to escape the monster now wreaking havoc throughout FURNISH.

How the hell did this creature get out of my drawing?

It's not real. I drew it from my imagination....

No time for that now, Yohan.

I begin to summon Aiden's Spiral.

It's finally time to put all that practice to good use.

Will it to spin, Yohan. Will it to spin.

The creature lunges at me, mouth dripping with saliva, growling loud, wings expanding, sending paperwork flying across the room.

I can feel the heat of its breath getting closer, its teeth exposed and threatening…

Spin for me. Please spiral! I will you to spin!

"YOHAN!"

"Wake up, you are going to be late for work!"

"Okay, Okay, I hear you! I'm up, Pa!"

…What a crazy ass dream.

Gross, I'm sweating like a pig.

I blink my eyes open, look at my phone, and realize I still have over an hour left before I have to be at the Torture Chamber. There's enough time to get ready, especially if I decide to grab a Dryve.

My dad stares at me for a brief moment before he turns around and starts to make his way out.

"¡Ay Dios Mio! When will this boy…"

I hear my father talking to himself as he exits my room. Guess I'm starting the day by disappointing him once again.

I can't think too hard about that. I have to get to my wonderful hell hole of a job.

I get ready quickly, take a fast shower, throw on my clothes for the day, and double-check to make sure I have my I.D. badge. Thanks to Lexie, I try to keep that thing close.

I order my Dryve and head down the stairs of my apartment.

I figure I'll wait outside. The day looked beautiful from my bedroom, and I could definitely use some sun as a pick me up after being alerted by Ella that I might have inadvertently marked myself for death last night.

What uplifting news.

I look down blankly at my arm.

Well, this tattoo might've had the exact opposite effect of what I was going for.

I'm leaning on the wall of our brick building, taking hits of my Cannapuffy, when I see a guy approaching. He looks like he's heading toward my apartment complex.

He's tall and kind of muscular with a haircut like mine, except the sides of his head are shaven, and he's missing the patch of blue, but the curls are there, sitting neatly groomed at the top of his head.

His style is a bit preppy and reminds me of those old-school surfer-type guys, but it works for him.

The ripped jeans and the tight polo shirt are complementing, and I can't stop my eyes from doing a thorough scan of his body.

My body and mind react in the same way at the same time.

He is... EVERYTHING.

He walks closer, and I try to avoid all eye contact. I'm incredibly awkward when it comes to talking to new people, especially guys.

I just never know how they are going to react to me.

Shit, he's coming to the door. Don't be weird, Yohan, don't be weird.

"Hey, Bro,"

"Uh, hi," I respond, voice shaky.

"You live here too? Or waiting for someone? I haven't seen you around."

"Yeah, that's probably because I'm new. I just moved here. I'm up on the third."

Maybe that's too much information, crap I'm doing it again... being awkward.

"Oh, cool, I'm on the first. I'm Nash, by the way."

He reaches out his hand, and I meet mine with his, hoping he'll ignore the pools of sweat now excreting from my palms.

"Yohan, but my friends call me Yo-Yo."

He shakes my hand and offers up the most alluring smile that makes me go completely warm inside.

"Well, nice to meet you, Yo-Yo."

I see my Dryve pulling up, and it couldn't be more than perfect timing.

I swear, if I stand here any longer, I am going to either faint or disappear altogether because this Nash guy's hypnotic-like energy is sending my anxiety through the roof.

"Nice to meet you too, Nash."

"That's my ride, gotta head out," I say with a nervous laugh.

Ugh, you freaking idiot; you are doing it again.

I point to the Dryve, now pulling up to the sidewalk.

"Okay, well, I'll see you around Yo-Yo."

He heads into the apartment building, and I can't lie. I couldn't help but stall for a minute to watch him walk away before I headed into my Dryve.

Yeah, right, Yohan, he's probably straight, and even if he wasn't, you could never get a guy like him.

As I sit in my Dryve and head to work, I switch the destination from FURNISH to Eat Your Heart Out Bakery. I'm going to surprise the girls with some snacks to thank them for being there for me when I needed someone.

It's always hard in a new place, and I never get used to it.

The bakery isn't far from our job, so once I have a bag full of sushi pie rolls, I start walking to work.

My thoughts are skipping around, per usual, as I make my way through the streets of Wellwash.

Hmm. Nash is an interesting name. I wonder if it's short for something.

...

I hope they like the rolls I picked.

...

I really hope I'm not stuck with another set of training videos again; my eyeballs were assaulted enough yesterday.

The walk went by super quickly, and I make my way into FUR-NISH through all the departments in the showroom before I run into my coworkers, Jaden and Rose.

"Hey, you're late, Yohan."

I look down at my watch.

"Only by five minutes. I just woke up a little late today."

"Had enough time to grab food, though, I see," Rose chimes in.

"Leave Yo-Yo alone..."

"...like let's get real here, Hunty's. You guys aren't even management, let alone supervisors, so just hop off his dick already. It's five minutes."

Rose and Jaden move to the side, and I now see Lexie standing there with her hand on her hip and eyebrow raised like she means business.

"Lexie, that's not work-appropriate language," Jaden says matter-of-factly.

"Yeah, since we are stating what we should and shouldn't be doing while at our jobs, according to the meeting we had last month, harassment is a no-no."

"Now, Yohan, do you feel like you are being harassed?"

"Is Mr. Micromanaging Jaden here harassing you?" she adds.

"No need to answer. Let's go. We've got official office furniture business to handle."

I walk through Jaden and Rose and can feel the tense energy, though they are absolutely silent. I guess Lexie kind of has that effect on people when she gets into what she calls her "bad bitch" mode.

We make our way to our department, and I spot Ella relaxing in one of the display office chairs.

She meets my gaze and rushes over to join me and Lexie.

"Omg, is that a bag from Eat Your Heart Out Bakery, I see?"

"It is."

I dangle the bag in the air, giving her a huge smile.

"I just wanted to get a little thank you for you guys for listening to me vent the other night. I figured we could maybe pop these in the fridge and have lunch together later?"

"Sounds like a plan." Says Lexie

"Yes, but let's call it brunch, Haus of Ascension brunch."

"Okay, it was cute at first, Ella Hun, but now you're overdoing it."

I immediately laugh; their back-and-forth banter is becoming quite iconic in my eyes, and I'm happy to be included.

The comradery doesn't last for long, though, because the customers pile in shortly after.

I tried my best to answer all the questions I could. I mean, you don't really get much hands-on learning from sitting on a computer taking quizzes about the products and services we offer. Still, I guess the essential customer interaction toolkit was there.

For the things I couldn't figure out on my own, I would reach out to Aella or Lexie and hopefully get a quick answer.

In all honesty, I am happy I made that stop to grab us lunch on the way here because I'm pretty sure I'm getting on their last nerves at this point from relying on them so much.

The clock ticks on by, and after being asked about lime green binders for what I think is about the fifteenth time, it's finally time to head to our breaks.

Lexie leads the way.

First, we stop by the lunchroom to grab our bag from the bakery and buy some drinks from the vending machine.

I was pulling up a chair like a complete idiot because I just assumed we would eat lunch in, you know, the lunchroom, but Lex and Ella apparently had other plans.

I follow Ella and Lexie out of the lunchroom and through the showroom to a side hallway that is entirely empty and has a sign marked Emergency Exit.

Please don't go off alarm.

Lexie pushes the door open and holds it for Ella to walk through, and I follow suit, utterly dumbfounded as to where we are going.

"And he's all like, well, your website said it was in stock, and I'm like, well, it's not."

"Omg, I hate that. Yo-Yo, don't you hate that?"

"Totally," I add.

We stride across the pavement of the parking lot, joking about our customer interactions for the day, until we finally reach a picnic table on a patch of grass a few feet away from the building.

"Welcome to the smoker's area." Says Ella.

"Before you ask, we're not out here to get high or satisfy our nico-tine cravings. We're here to escape the *others*, you know, coworkers like Jaden."

"He's so freaking annoying. You know he asked me if I'm ever going to consider coming to work without a tie?"

"I'm like, are you ever going to get out of my ass?"

"Yeah, he's always up everyone's ass. Yohan, is he up your ass too?"

"Last time I checked, no."

"Okay, well, I wasn't sure because climbing up asses is his favorite pastime."

"Hashtag, clench your cheeks."

We all roll into laughter and start grabbing our sushi rolls out of the bag.

I pick at my roll, and it gets silent with everyone focused on chewing and killing the hunger -currently dwelling in us from the weight of the day.

Should I say something or wait for them to bring it up?...

"So are we just going to act like you didn't send a text last night saying you think Yohan here is going to die because of this Aiden's Spiral tattoo thing or..."

Thank You, outspoken Lexie.

"Well, I delivered the message. I was waiting for one of you guys to bring it up."

I can't help but take this opportunity to voice my opinion.

"Yeah, so was I, to be honest, but since we're on the topic..."

"...in the spirit of being prepared for, you know, whatever the hell we're preparing for, I tried to practice Aiden's Spiral, the summoning, or whatever you wanna call it, and.... nothing happened."

"Yeah, well, I wouldn't think you'd master it in a few hours...I mean, if it's even a thing."

"Good point..." Ella adds.

She continues.

"...but I was thinking...."

Lexie and I both drop our rolls midway to our mouths.

Oh gosh, my intuition is kicking in. This is probably not good.

"...we should try the simple wishing thing; it wouldn't hurt, and we all have stuff we want, right? Things we could wish for to enhance our lives a bit? Or... I guess we could just wish for protection from whatever we need to be protected from?"

Me and Lexie look at each other for what seems like forever.

I mean, I could use a life upgrade, and this shit probably isn't real, anyway.

Well, according to Max, it is, and to be honest, I kind of believe it too.

I wonder what Bash would think... should I even tell him?

I mean...

"Uh, hello, you guys!"

"I'm in," I say without really thinking much more about it.

"Whelp. Majority rules, so I guess we're doing witchcraft now, apparently."

"Yay, Haus of Ascension, it's about to get real."

She puts a firm fist up in the air.

"Yeah, real annoying...."

"Ella, what did I tell you about that crap?"

"I don't know, I kind of like it," I add.

"Oh, here we go. Ella's got a cosigner."

We laugh and continue our lunch at the table until it's finally time to head back into what Lexie calls the *Torture Chamber*.

The rest of the workday went by as expected. The customers were still annoying, and I still lacked the answers to most of their questions.

By the time it was time to go, I was completely exhausted. I worked out the details of my plans with Lexie and Ella and decided to take a Dryve home.

I was too tired to walk, and I think I've seen enough of Wellwash now to get around. The awe has kind of dissipated at this point. There's not really much left to see.

As I exit my Dryve, I see a guy leaning on the wall by the entrance of my building.

None other than Nash, the guy I met earlier.

The hot one.

Ugh, not now. I'm tired.

When do my witchcraft powers start kicking in?

I want to be invisible, just walk right past this guy, skip the anxiety, the awkwardness, the searching for words...

"Hey, Yo-Yo." He says in the most casual tone.

Damn that voice.

"Uh... Hey, Nash."

"Do you mind swiping me in? I forgot my fob."

Do you mind bringing the fantasy I'm secretly having about you to life right now?

"Um, yeah, no problem. One sec."

I place my fob on the door, hear it unlock, and grab the handle, motioning for him to walk in first.

I just couldn't resist the opportunity to check him out again without him noticing.

I follow his lead, and he stops in the hallway as the door shuts.

Oh crap, he caught me.

"I hope this doesn't seem weird, but I can't help but notice all of your tattoos."

Oh, Thank God.

"No, not weird. They are all out there on display, and I get questions about them like every day."

I chuckle nervously.

"I see, ha-ha...Well, I was just wondering, I'm looking to get a piece done, maybe a tribal..., I was thinking maybe you could recommend someone to me or something."

I notice him place his hand behind his head and get all fidgety.

Is this really happening? Is this guy nervous to talk to ME?

Is this an attempt at hitting on ME?

What is happening?

"Umm, I kind of got them all in different places. I move around a lot. It's my dad..."

"...he's a traveling nurse. I wouldn't really know anywhere around here..."

He interrupts.

"Well, maybe you can help me pick a design. I like your ink. It's pretty badass."

"Yeah, I mean, I draw. Most of the things I like are kind of influenced by metal or fantasy, but..."

He cuts me off...again.

"That's perfect."

"Here, take my number."

We exchange numbers and make a bit of small talk about potential designs, and it's getting slightly easier to talk to him.

Maybe because he's doing most of the talking, but hell, I'll take it.

When our conversation ends, I finally make my way up the stairs and into my apartment to get out of my work clothes, shower, and get ready for bed.

Once I've settled in for the night, I grab my laptop, prop it on my bed, and sign into my messenger quickly to see if Bash is online.

My question is quickly answered when I notice that the chat bubble is still gray, and the status icon shows he hasn't logged in since the last time we talked.

I'm getting a little worried since our last conversation wasn't the best, but I can only hope that he is okay and will check first thing in the morning to see if he's back online again.

I lay my head back on my headboard, still wide awake and slightly anxious.

I can't sleep. The thoughts keep popping in and out of my head like little soldiers stationed around my brain with the sole purpose of defending me from sleep.

Worried thoughts about Bash.

The not-so-P.G. thoughts about Nash.

Ha-ha, Bash and Nash.

The most commanding thought, though...

The one I can't get out of my mind... is the thought that I might be getting into some crazy shit.

I'm about to do witchcraft beyond the stuff I tried from the message boards and with other people...

What is that called like a coven?

Am I in a coven now?

Hell, I might be in a mini cult.

No, that's not a thing?

Is it a thing?

Whatever the case may be, I'll find out the truth tomorrow, and all the speculation will be put to rest.

Just three sort of kind of maybe witches...

Or two witches and a warlock?

Just over here casting a wishing spell...

...A wishing spell

Wait a minute...

Why are none of us concerned about who sent that damn email?

Who could've possibly sent that email?

CHAPTER SEVEN

Lexie

"**Y**OU KNOW YOU REALLY are my best friend..."

"...you just get me. It's like fate, you know..."

"Anthony..."

My mother proceeds to scream down the hall.

"Your crazy daughter is in here professing her love to one of her bottles again. She's gone mad."

"Sorry, Mom, I didn't see you there. I thought I locked my door."

I laugh nervously while gently tossing my cookie dough whiskey onto my now neatly made bed.

"You know, I was just having a little cleaning sesh, bringing in some fresh energy, some good vibes."

"Yeah, I've been here for a minute, watching your crazy performance. Maybe you should've gone to a school for the arts. Probably would've been your thing."

"She's not crazy; she's an artist." My sister Xyla spins into the room with her magnifying glass in hand.

Yeah, my door was definitely not locked.

"Wow, your room is super clean. Are you expecting company?"

I kneel to meet her at eye level and place my hand on her shoulder.

"You are going to be the world's best detective one day, I swear," I respond, throwing her a wink.

"Ella coming over?... Please behave responsibly, you guys. I don't need a repeat of last time."

My mother gives me a stern look. I'm pretty sure I would've sat through a rehashing of every detail of Ella's drunken display on her last visit if my sister wasn't currently present.

We didn't drink that much, but sometimes a shot or two is too much for that girl.

"Yeah, Ella and my new coworker. His name is Yohan, and he's pretty cool. He's an artist, and don't worry, we're actually just going to try this new meditation I saw online. He's into manifesting, too."

"Oh my gosh, I wanna manifest! I want that new phone, the one that's see-through and lights up when you get notifications."

"Now, Xyla, you know manifesting is just like praying..."

My mom throws me yet another serious look.

Manifesting and the practice of meditation are not forms of devil worship. Mom, get with the times.

"...just pray for the things you want; before you know it, they will come to you."

"Oh yeah? I've been praying for weeks and have yet to..."

My mom leads Xyla out of my bedroom with the most exaggerated smile, and she continues to rant about everything she wants to change about her life.

"Remember what I said. Behave responsibly."

She gives me a glance that shows she means business and shuts my bedroom door.

Ugh, that was a lot.

I continue to organize my room, cleaning things up and making it presentable.

If there's one thing I've learned from all of these *"change your life"* type videos, it's that creating a clean and inviting space is essential for a positive outcome.

I admit I might've overdone it, but I couldn't help myself.

I had the day off today, so I went and got things I thought we might need, budget-friendly items, of course.

A girl is broke.

I thought candles would be appropriate, but the only ones on sale were Midnight Kiss…, so I guess we're getting romantic with the wishing tonight.

In addition to the candles, I picked up some incense and a crystal kit I saw in the home décor section.

I looked them up, and they're supposedly quartz, which is the magical equivalent of all-purpose from what I've gathered.

I'm a newbie. How the hell am I supposed to know what I'm doing?

I don't even know why we're doing it in MY house.

What if there's a lingering spirit here or something?

The movies have warned me about this sort of thing.

Just as I'm growing impatient, waiting for Ella and Yohan to finally get here, I hear my phone go off, and I'm excited but nervous in anticipation of what's about to go down.

Ella

We're outside.

I leave my room and head down the stairs to our front door to greet Ella and Yohan and show them up to my bedroom.

I decide to take a detour to the kitchen so my parents can meet Yohan and say hi to Ella before we start this séance thing or whatever we're doing.

The last thing I need is them walking in on that.

The greeting is casual and lasts about five minutes, and we make our way to my room.

"Oh, my goodness, it was totally hard looking them in the eye after I was stumbling all over their kitchen the last time I was here. Hopefully, they forgot."

"Ha-ha, you wish, girl. It's okay, though. You're basically like family. You had a moment, who hasn't?"

I go over to my dresser, grab my supplies, the candles, the crystals, the incense and take a seat on the floor right on my comfy shag carpet and get settled in.

"Cool room. You know I didn't take you for a girl who would like CorpseSmash," Yohan says as he takes a seat next to me, pointing to a poster on my wall.

"What, you never seen a Caribbean girl twerk to some metal? I know all about getting up with the illness."

"Besides, I have quite the reputation for turning it out in a mosh honey. You better ask about me."

I flip my pink hair to the side and show off my booty-popping skills.

"Yeah, Yo-Yo were eclectic ass bitches. Get with it." Ella snaps her fingers and plops down on the floor.

I guess this is our definition of forming a circle.

"Have you guys thought about what you're going to wish for?" I ask, genuinely curious.

Yohan jumps at the opportunity to answer this question as quickly as he can like it has been the only thought he's had all day.

"Well, I was thinking, since we know I'm not the one who sent this email, Ahem, I'm hoping we've gotten past that thought by now..."

He looks at Ella, then me.

"We have," she says.

"We have," I add.

"Okay, good, because once again, it wasn't me..."

"...that being said, I was thinking maybe I would wish that we could find out who actually sent the email..."

"...seems like a good use for a wish. It might not solve our problem, but at least we'll know where to go from there."

What a brilliant idea. Why didn't I think of that?

"Omg, yes, I've tried everything I could. I even tried to send a reply to the email, but every time, the email address shows up with asterisks, or I get an automatic reply that says the message could not be delivered."

"Ok, so, one wish down. What about you, Ella?"

She looks down at the floor, biting her lip and fidgeting with her tie.

This time, she's sporting the one with the little gummy bears dancing.

I love this one.

"Um, so first, I have a confession, you guys." She says, still not looking up from the floor.

I swear if she says she's the one who sent this email, I am going to SCREAM.

I look at Yohan, and he seems like he might be thinking the same thing, but before I can respond, he shares his opinion.

"We're in this together, remember? I know Lexie's here for you, and so am I, so tell us, what's up?"

She finally picks her head up and looks at Yohan, then at me, and I feel it coming.

Here's the confession.

"I kind of, sort of have my own little magic thing I do too..."

Okay, I'm confused. What the hell is she talking about? Little magic thing she does?

What? Changing ties?

"... so, Yohan, you admitted you did your research and dabbled with things a bit online..."

He looks at me and back at her.

"Uh-huh."

"...and Lexie, you do your meditation and manifesting stuff..."

"Wait, what?" Yohan looks over at me and raises his eyebrow curiously.

"Oh my God, it's nothing..."

"... just stuff from MeView to get my mind right. There are hundreds of channels about this stuff. It's harmless, just stuff for good vibes."

Eh, I guess I see how I could look guilty here, like I could be a suspect, too, setting this all up for shits and giggles.

Spoiler alert. I'm not.

"You mean to tell me you and Ella here were grilling me and looking at me like a crazy person when I tell you about my interest in the unknown while you're over here, trying your own attempt at magic?"

"Yohan, please, can we skip the pot and kettle? You are taking away from Ella's moment."

I redirect my attention to Ella, who is just sitting there observing now with her mouth shut.

"You were saying, Ella?"

I give Yohan a look, which I'm hoping translates clearly as *shut the hell up.*

"Well, I kind of watch and do tarot, okay, it's not a big deal," she says, rushing her words.

Of course, here goes Yohan again.

A day or two ago, the guy wouldn't say anything but generic comments, and now, by some utter miracle, he's absolutely full of conversation.

"Okay, so your email says you were chosen, and we all have dabbled in something magical. This all must mean this was supposed to happen... right?"

"...is anyone else getting that?"

"I mean, it makes sense," I respond.

I mean, he is making sense.

"It does," Ella adds.

"You doing tarot is super cool, actually. I wish you would've told me sooner; I would totally have had you reading my cards like all the time."

"Yeah, I wouldn't mind knowing what the future has in store for me, either."

I can see her getting excited, like she finally gets to share this little detail about herself she's kept tucked away for so long, and it makes me so happy for her.

"I'm not even that good, you guys, but I do know a lot of MeView readers that have my loyalty as a viewer, and I'd be happy to give you readings or share their info with you!"

"Okay, awesome, but we are completely sidetracking here."

"Ella Hun, What's your wish?"

"Yeah, I know you've got something cool in mind after that confession."

She looks down at the floor again. God, this girl.

"So, I was thinking, maybe I would wish to be able to see into the future, like become psychic. If that's a real thing, I'm just thinking…"

"…I want to try something out of the ordinary. If this is real, I want proof."

"I freaking love that! My best friend, the psychic."

I stare off at my ceiling, getting lost in a quick mini daze, thinking about all the potential advantages this could come with.

"Now I want something cool to wish for."

"Yeah, you made my wish sound boring."

I straighten my face, mimicking the expression my mother is best known for, so he knows I am absolutely serious.

"No, Yohan, you are keeping yours."

"Okay, Lexie, the boss lady, well, what's your wish then?"

"I guess I'm stuck with wishing for protection. That's what we agreed upon originally, right?"

"True," Yohan responds.

"Aww, how selfless Lexie, our hero," Ella says, now blinking her eyes dramatically.

Now that we've worked out the kinks, I decide to get us all set up so we can get this thing started.

Our séance or whatever.

I lay out the crystals in a circle around us and place the candles in points of four to represent the directions and elements like I saw in that movie about those witches a while back.

Hey, a reference is a reference.

I sit back in my position, place the incense holder in the center of the circle, and light it.

"All right, here we go. Everyone memorized what we're supposed to be doing here?"

"Yup."

"All set."

I center my mind like I learned from the MeView videos and shut my eyes, focusing on my breathing.

Inhale for 5, hold for 3, exhale slowly.

I visualize the three of us together, with a protective aura of rainbow light enveloping us, keeping us protected and providing the feeling of absolute safety.

Inhale for 5, hold for 3, exhale slowly.

I envision dark smoke-filled clouds attempting to break into our protective bubble, but they bounce away. They stand no chance.

We are too strong.

We stand in confidence.

I chant...

"We are always protected, we are always protected, we are always protected."

I try not to break concentration, keeping my focus on the force field of energy building up in my mind, but I can hear Yohan and Ella join in.

"The future is clear to me, the future is clear to me, the future is clear to me."

"The identity is revealed, the identity is revealed, the identity is revealed."

"We are protected..."

"The future is clear..."

"The identity is revealed..."

We somehow fall in sync after all our chanting of our specific desires...

We say the words of power.

"Aya Releaze, I-Din, Aya Releaze!".

I expect the walls to shake, the room to spin, a mist to appear.

But nope, nothing, absolutely nothing.

No spirits popping up giving us information on the email...

No, Ella making a stunning face, alerting us she's had a premonition...

So, I'm also guessing there's no way to verify we've even been granted protection, either. Great, just great.

I'm feeling like this is pointless, and I'm getting ready to bring my efforts to a halt, but that's when I hear it.

The candle to the left of me crackles, then pops.

I open my eyes and were all staring at each other cluelessly. Yeah, that was a coincidence, pure coincidence.

The candle then outs.

"Oh shit," I blurt out, at a loss for any other words.

Crackle, pop, out.

The remaining candles follow the same pattern, and I'm starting to get a little scared, but the light's still on, so there's a bit of hope.

"Ha-ha, you guys, minor detail. I forgot to fill you in on—"

"...these candles were on sale. They were practically giving them away, probably just a bad batch."

"Omg, Lex, you could've said that earlier. I almost had a heart attack over here, thinking demons were going to pop out or something, geez."

"Right, and here I am thinking we're getting all mystical and shit like the sender of the email was going to materialize, and we would have all the answers."

We all have a good laugh, and I pick up the candles and crystals, and we disassemble the circle we formed in the middle of my bedroom floor.

We've all moved to different spots in my room. I'm hanging out on my bed. Ella has taken comfort in my desk swivel chair, compliments of FURNISH, and Yohan is right at home, leaning on my wall, playing up his cool guy attitude.

"So, Yohan, Mr. Yo-Yo, Ella had mentioned to me you had a reason for your nickname, or like a story behind how you got it..."

"... you never told me."

"Oh, ha-ha, it's not that interesting really... I got it back when I lived in Shipton. My mom and dad were trying to work it out, so my dad took more jobs there for a period of time, at least when he could..."

"... my friends said I would go away and come back, you know, like a yo-yo, so it kind of stuck with me over the years."

"Aww, omg, that's so sweet. I love it. No more calling you Yohan. It's Yo-Yo from now on."

"Isn't it a cute story? When he first told me, I was like, I'm definitely going to like this guy."

"Was that before or after you thought I was a serial killer with a spiral trademark?"

"Ha-ha, fair, but honestly, the more I think about it..."

"...your name really fits, especially since you're here now in Well-wash as the Aiden's Spiral master. Ha-ha, the spiral spins just like a yo-yo."

"Oh my gosh, Lex, you're right. Is this fated or what?"

I reach under my pillow, my favorite hiding place for my dear friend Ms. Cookie Dough Whiskey.

"How about we celebrate with a round of shots?"

"...to debunking this email, which was obviously a load of crap, and to a new solid friendship of almost could have been witches."

"Heck, yes!" Ella agrees.

"I'm always down," Yo-Yo adds as he finally peels himself off my wall, and we all stand again in a circle, passing the bottle around and taking swigs.

"Well, so much for psychic predictions. I was actually looking forward to that," I say as I take another large gulp from my bottle of whiskey.

I can barely get the shot down when the lights in my room start to flicker and then go completely out.

My TV powers on with a loud thunderous sound, and grainy black-and-white pixels take over my 43-inch monitor.

The picture blurs, then turns clear, and I am now staring at a young blond woman with perfectly straight hair, a low-cut shirt, and bright green eyes.

She looks like the token popular girl, like the head sorority sister or the boss at work who serves up just the right amount of sarcasm to not get in trouble but still get under your skin.

She looks at each of us individually and then smiles, displaying her gleaming white and pearly perfect teeth.

"Hola bitches, you ready to get magical?"

What the hell?

CHAPTER Eight

Lexie

"H ELLO?"

"You guys?"

"Damnit, Reggie, I told you to check the audio and ensure it was all set before we launched this..."

"...you had one job, and you can't even freaking..."

"We can totally hear you." Yohan interrupts what I assume would have been the chewing out of her friend, who must be somewhere in the background hiding and apparently in charge of audio for extensive reveals/room invasions.

She pauses and turns back, facing the camera again, giving a stiff smile, and we all look at each other just as confused as we were when she first popped onto my TV screen. Out of nowhere, in the middle of my bedroom.

Who is this girl?

"Yeah, so just sit there and make me look stupid, you guys, that's a great way to start out…"

"…whatever…as I was saying…"

"Hey, witches…"

"…I'm Madison, a mostly rogue tech witch, but I do have my posse per se, or, as you guys like to call it, a house?"

"Or Haus… to be fancy, I assume…"

"…either way…I like it, it's… cute…"

A voice from the background chimes in, "Really, Maddie?… your rogue… yeah, because we're just insignificant little beings over here."

She gives a snarky look to the camera and turns to address one of her *friends* in the background.

"The most powerful pages were sent to me. I think that's a clear indication as to who runs the show around here. You two knuckleheads need me more than I need you…"

"…I would keep that at the forefront of your simple little thoughts and reconsider your snapbacks and interruptions if I were you."

She clicks her tongue and whips her head back to face the camera.

"He-he, so hard to find a decent clique these days; everyone's so… rude."

I can't help but stare at this girl. I'm at a loss for words. She's giving me everything I don't like, the bitchy attitude, the know-it-all demeanor, and a tech witch?

Then why the hell is her background filled with teddy bears and grossly overly pink?

Shouldn't she have, like, several wires and plugs running all over with dual monitors displaying lines of cryptic code or sketchy-looking software… whatever a tech witch would use…

"Okay, so do you guys like talk or what? Obviously, your new witches, casting spells without magical wards to go undetected... that's so rudimentary."

"I clearly can't be the only witch that's picked up on your vibes... but gauging your responses to me, or lack thereof... I must be the first... either that or you guys are extremely lost..."

"Yeah, lost... confused, all the above..." Ella chimes in.

"I, for one, am not lost. I can already tell Ms. Madison, the self-proclaimed tech sorceress over here, probably doesn't have our best interest in mind..."

Yohan looks at me, then Ella, waiting for a response.

We're both silent.

In my mind, having someone who has the slightest bit of an idea of what's going on in our back pocket doesn't seem like a bad idea at all, considering, at this point, we know absolutely nothing.

I have no idea what Ella is thinking, and she's yet to voice her opinion, but I can only hope her thoughts align with mine, or at least somewhere close.

Madison continues.

It appears she's under the impression that her grand entrance is still ongoing.

"Au contraire doll face, if anything, I should be an ally..."

"...you newbies don't look like you know any other witches, so I'm what you should consider valuable... for knowledge and experience, of course."

Ella breaks her silence.

"Wait... back up a bit... how did you know we call ourselves a Haus?"

"How funny... the redhead acting like a blonde."

She starts laughing hysterically while we all try to figure out what the hell is so hilarious.

"Reggie! Hun, be sure to timestamp this part for later, for when I need a good laugh, they are so basic..."

"...Your Aella, right?"

"Yeah."

"...Ha-ha, well, Ella, as I mentioned, all about ten seconds ago... I am a tech witch..."

"...and because I specialize in technology, I did some research on you guys, nothing big, just sifting through messages and apps just to get to know you a bit, some more than others..."

She throws Yohan a wink, and I want to gag instantly.

He won't be into you, girl; even if he were, he just wouldn't.

"...you really should value yourself more, Mr. Yohan. It's really not a good idea to send those types of pictures to people on the internet for free. You need to make them work for it, babes."

I turn to Yohan, who is now absolutely bright red, and now this girl is really pissing me off.

How dare you come into my room, insult my friends, and think you are some sort of elite individual?

Guess what, Madison, you are about to see who the top-notch bitch really is.

Okay, Lexie, it's time to let this chick have it.

I take a sip of my cookie dough whiskey and toss the bottle on my bed, ready for war.

"Listen, MADISON, check your shit... because we here..."

I motion towards Yo-Yo and Ella, who are now watching with anticipation of what comes next.

"...new or not, will not be disrespected..."

"... and I don't care what or who you know, the message said *we* were chosen, which means *we* have power too, so unless you want a magical ass whooping, I would fix your tone."

Her facial expression shifts almost instantly.

She's no longer laughing or finding any of this comical... she is angry.

She adjusts her position in her chair.

"I don't take well to threats, Lexie. Furthermore, what good is having power if you don't know how to use it?"

"I didn't come here with the intention to start drawing lines in the sand... but seeing how you were the first to grab the stick..."

"... consider it game on, bitch."

"Is the name-calling necessary?" Ella says in what I think is an attempt to make peace.

"It isn't Ella, darling, and I'm more than happy to work with you; at least you have respect..."

I'll show you respect. You're lucky your ass is on a TV screen right now.

"See, Ella, I'm only here because I need you guys to will me your pages..."

"...that's it, it's pretty simple, just will them to me and I'll be gone... just like that *snap*, it'll be... magical."

She giggles, and it's annoying.

"Didn't you say you went through our phones? You would've seen the messages..."

"... and now that I think more about it, you said you sensed our magic. It's only been about forty-five minutes. How the hell could you go through all our messages..."

Madison chuckles once again.

"I really don't have time to explain everything to you, but here's the gist..."

"... the concept of time is manmade, magic trumps that façade... and I can absorb knowledge fairly quickly, especially through technology. I think I've mentioned that before... keeping up, girl?"

Ella nods, and I know her obedient behavior is feeding Madison's ravenous ego the gobs and gobs of attention it needs, and it's driving me nuts.

Rough her up a bit, Ella. I know you have it in you.

"...that being said, I cannot have the pages unless they are willed to me. They are magically encrypted and can only be read by those who are meant to see them, unless they are willed, or you know the recipient is killed... but I'd prefer not to go that route... too messy."

She fidgets with her nails, which, of course, are also pink.

"Try it, I dare you. You're not getting a damn thing from us." I can't help but lash out a response. She wants someone to be scared, and I'm nowhere near intimidated, not even slightly.

"I was talking to Ella..."

Yohan clears his throat, bringing the attention to himself.

"What is the point of all this? Why do you even want the pages? If we will them to you, what happens? To you? To us?"

"...As I said before, I don't have time for all these questions. Are you going to will me the pages or not?... and this time, I'm talking to you, pink-haired girl."

"And as I said before, NO!"

"...now get the hell out of my room or off my TV, whatever the hell, just get out."

"So be it, but don't think this is over..."

"...it's a game, after all, honey, and I just love games... Toodles."

She sticks both her middle fingers up at the camera, and the screen goes just as black as it was before.

"She's the utter manifestation of every personality trait I absolutely detest."

I can't help but express my true feelings about my brief introduction to Madison. I don't know how anyone else is feeling, but I don't like that girl, not one bit. I don't care if she has the knowledge anymore; everything in my body is telling me to avoid her at all costs.

"I know…" Ella comments.

"…she kept insisting that I was stupid, but I mean, I was in shock; stuff like this doesn't happen to me every day. What was I supposed to do?"

"Screw her, you're not stupid, Ella. You had questions, as we all did. She needs someone to knock her off her high horse, and she met the right one!"

I am fuming. I can't believe she was as insulting as she was, especially considering the fact that she invaded my personal space with no invitation, just intrusion and rudeness.

She ruined my buzz, and no one gets away with ruining my buzz.

"Okay, you guys, I know Madison wasn't the kindest person. Trust me, I dislike her too, but she did give us some clues as to what we're up against…"

Of course, Mr. magic-obsessed Yohan would be focusing on the witchcraft of it all.

"… I mean, she said she sensed our magic because we weren't using wards or whatever she called it, so that means we must've done something, triggered something."

"You're right. She did say that. Does that mean I'm going to become psychic?"

"If so, I have major plans. This is so exciting; I don't feel any different, though. What if we failed, but she just sensed us trying?"

I go back for my whiskey bottle and take a swig, trying to erase the feeling of annoyance Madison has now imprinted on my energy.

"Anything is possible at this point, is how I feel. It's getting weird. If a random girl can pop up on my TV screen in the middle of my room, who knows what the heck is next? For all I know, this could become a daily event. All I know is that the email says we're chosen, so we can handle this."

I try to remind them that we are powerful too; it's just a matter of finding out how to wield this power, and since we're in it deep now, I, Lexie Smith, am one hundred percent committed.

"Listen, you guys, we're in this, fully in this. We can't be afraid. Come on, her room was filled with teddy bears and painted pink. If we're going to have an arch nemesis or whatever we should call the opposing side... she's obviously level one..."

"... we can get through all of this. We just need to figure out how."

"You're right, Lex, we got this. We have at least some pages. That's a start..."

Yohan interrupts.

"True Ells..."

Ew... Ells. No. Not a thing.

"... but what could the other pages have that ours doesn't? We have the spiral, a wishing spell, and a warning, which were obviously past at this point..."

I have to interject because, once again, I feel like we're getting lost in the things we don't know instead of piecing together what we do.

"Ella, Yo-Yo, listen to me, please..."

I move closer to them, plant my feet firmly on the ground, straighten my back, and position my head forward to project a sense of dominance in this little magical discussion.

"... we have what we have, and we are going to do what we need to do... to stay protected, to find an exit from all of this, to find answers..."

"...if I'm being honest, I don't even know *what* we are doing or what the point of all of this is, but what I do know is that we will figure it all out, we won't fail, we can't ...we will win..."

"...if manifestation and meditation have taught me anything, it's that the mind state has full control..."

"... believe, and it will come to fruition. We will win."

"I like that, we will, we have to," Yohan affirms confidently.

"Yeah, I've survived being a triplet for twenty-two years, so this has to be a cakewalk."

"Wait, you're a triplet?"

You would've thought Ella had mentioned that. I think it's a fun fact, and if it were me, I'd say it every chance I got.

I need to avoid us sidetracking again; it seems to be our thing, so I bring attention back to what we truly need to focus on.

"Alright, you guys, so it's settled..."

"...operation take down Madison, the tech demon witch girl, in full effect. We just need to dig into the information we have so far a little bit deeper..."

"...maybe Yo-Yo, you can try to reach out to your friend Max or that guy Zeus, and Ella, maybe try to consult with your cards or online readers?"

"You really think that tarot will help us?" Ella says, with a glimmer in her eye.

"I think we're beyond questioning the supernatural right now. We need to use the resources we have."

"I think it's a great start," Yohan adds, reaching for my whiskey.

Okay, things are starting to feel back to normal, or at least as normal as it can be for what we are currently dealing with.

I gave my pep talk. At least I did the best I could, but admittedly, I'm still annoyed, annoyed with the fact that I am the one who somehow has inadvertently taken the position of leader, although Mr. Yo-Yo here seems to know more than I do about this witchcraft-type stuff.

At this point, this is becoming a second job that I doubt I can list on my resume.

"Yeah, and there just must be more to it. The pages must be given to certain people for a reason. Why did we get the ones we did? There has to be..."

Before I can even finish my sentence, I hear two pings, one from my phone and the second from my laptop.

Yohan and Ella both look at me curiously.

For goodness' sake, Madison, can you at least give us a moment to process all of this?

I just know it's her.

The three people I've been talking to the most these past few days are right here with me.

My parents and sister are home, so who else could it be?

It's Madison. I know it is.

I reach for my phone and open the notifications.

It's not Madison.

It's another email.

Chapter Nine

Aella

"WHAT IS IT? WHAT is she saying now?"

God, can this girl give us a few minutes to process some of this? She just popped up out of nowhere and threatened us, and now she's texting? Good Greif.

I notice the confused look on Lexie's face, and I'm wondering what she could have possibly said to her. It can't be more shocking than the back-and-forth we all endured a second ago.

"It's not Madison. It's a reply from that weird email address."

"Omg, what does it say?"

"Yeah, Lex, did it work? Do we know who it's from?"

"All it says is my application is still under review."

"Your application?" I ask, confused.

"Yeah, I don't know you guys. Remember, I told you this all started when I sent applications for a new job? The original email came in as a reply to one of my applications. I'm assuming this is a response to whatever the hell we did with that spell or wish we cast. I know it doesn't make much sense, but what really does anymore?"

Yohan starts to scratch his head, his face illustrating a look of frustration. "Yeah, you could be right. Actually, I hope you are because, in that case, that would mean the protection aspect of the wishing spell must have had an effect, too, and we could use all the help we can get right now."

I can't help but ask more questions.

"So, still under review? Does that mean it will be revealed when we pass some sort of test? Like this is a trial run or something? That there's more to figure out? I mean, clearly, there is, but I'm just trying to wrap my head around this."

"I'm just as confused as you, Ella. I still don't even fully understand how this whole thing started, and why me? Why us? And isn't magic supposed to be fun? This is not fun so far. Not fun at all."

I start to get lost in my thoughts. As Yohan said, if the email response worked, then the protection would have increased for us somehow, which means I should also be getting my wish.

I don't feel any different, and I haven't had any increase in intuition or inkling to make one choice or another that could help us figure any of this out.

Maybe it takes time, or maybe I'm thinking too hard; perhaps this is an ideal time to consult the cards.

My thoughts are interrupted by Yohan's input.

"Well, I think we did a good job, if you ask me."

Lexie and I focus our gazes on Yohan, both raising an eyebrow.

"Did we?" I ask, unsure of what he is referring to.

"Yeah, I mean, think about it. We've all seen those movies, right? The ones with the witches who discover new powers and wish for money, or love, or fame, you know, the usual glamorous stuff life has to offer…"

I can't help but chuckle because I think I know where he is going with this.

"… and they end up with someone dying and getting an inheritance, or people becoming so obsessed with them that they would literally kill to be with them."

"Or actually kill them if they can't have them for themselves," Lexie adds.

"Yeah, exactly. We skipped the parts that would give any negative outcome, so, in my opinion, we're already bad asses. If Madison wants to label herself the tech sorceress, then we are most definitely the intellectuals."

"Yes, we'll magically whoop your ass with our brains."

Yohan and Lexie look at each other and laugh, and I am happy the mood changes. It was getting a bit dense in here after Madison's intrusion, and I could use some uplifting.

"But honestly, I never understood those witches in those movies… I mean, where on earth did you expect the money to come from? And love? Love is so overrated. Who needs it? All I need is Ms. Cookie Dough here, and a girl is all set."

She wiggles the whiskey bottle in the air.

"Oh, come on, Lex, everyone wants love, right Yo-Yo? Tell her."

"I kind of agree with both of you. Overrated, yes, but love would be cool, I guess. I never really been in what I would call an *actual* relationship."

"Wait, what?"

Really? Never?

I'm just as shocked as Lexie, but I think my face hides it way better.

"I've dated, of course, but nothing that I would consider *real*, only because I was doing it just to do it, you know? I never really felt invested."

"That's normal, Hun, and we've all been there. Tell him Ella."

"Been there, done that, got a couple of the tee shirts."

Yohan snorts a laugh and signals to Lexie for Ms. Cookie Dough. He takes a shot and continues.

"Funny story actually, now that this is happening, this whole magical adventure we're on reminds me of something I did when I was younger, from a movie I watched, but it was stupid..."

"Omg, tell us," I say now, taking a tiny sip of whiskey myself and getting comfy on Lexie's shag carpet.

"Yes, spill the beans, Mr. Yo-Yo."

"...Okay, well, I saw this movie once, and these witches were casting spells for love. I always knew I was considered *different* since I was a kid and that the chances of me finding love would be against the odds anyway, so I figured, what the hell..."

"Uh huh, Uh Huh,"

"... so, in the movie, one of the witches wished for a boyfriend who had physical characteristics that were highly unlikely to occur naturally, so I played with that idea a little and made a wish of my own and did a spell I found in a book from the library."

"You were just witching around since birth, huh?"

I burst out laughing. The combination of whiskey and Lexie's humor always gets me.

"Well, what did you ask for your potential love to look like?" I ask.

"Well, I didn't ask for him to look like anything specifically; I just asked him to bring me something that I knew didn't exist in real life because I knew I would never find him, and if I did, the only explanation had to be magic."

"Aww, Yohan, you're breaking my heart, Hun. You will find love one day, don't worry, and I know it sounds crazy coming from the girl who just said it was overrated, but if that's what you want, trust me, you'll find it."

"You will, but out of curiosity, what did you ask him to bring you?" I ask, genuinely curious.

"A black rose."

"I said I would know if he brought me a black rose. Won't see that coming anytime soon."

"Well, that was before you met us. Now, we are a powerhouse making wishes happen! That black rose might be closer than you think."

"I agree with Lexie here, and I mean we can always revisit it if you want, after we figure out what we're doing and all, not that you need magic for love or anything, but hey, I might want to try it myself, a girl's got needs."

"And side note, black roses technically do exist, just not naturally, so that ups your chances significantly."

We spend another half hour coming up with theories about what this all means while checking our phones periodically on the watch for Madison before we decide to call it a night, and I catch a Dryve home where I take time to gather my many thoughts.

Who is this Madison girl, and why does she want these pages so badly?

What could possibly be on the other pages... and who has the entire book? This Book of Ascension?

If they have the entire book, wouldn't that mean they have all the knowledge to become top-notch in the afterlife or whatever Yohan was talking about?

What's the point of sending out a few pages to people here and there?

What are we really up against?

The Dryve finally pulls up to the front of my apartment, and I exit the car without paying much attention to the driver and make my way to the front door while I search my bag for my key.

I really just want to get some sleep and tackle everything tomorrow.
My brain is on overload.

I finally find my key, insert it into the door, and head inside, letting out an exhausted breath.

As I make my way through the hallway that leads to the kitchen, I notice my brothers, Aedan and Aesher, sitting at the kitchen table, which is unprecedented since the two are barely ever home. I get a gut feeling they are waiting for me, and I can't help but think, what now?

Aesher stands up and pulls out a chair while Aeden gestures for me to take a seat.

"Hey, sis, how was your day?" Aeden asks with the worst fake and forced smile, I really hope he doesn't think he's pulling off the everything is okay vibe he's currently trying to serve.

"Okay, you guys, I've had a day, so let's cut the shit. We're triplets, remember? Kind of like twins, the telepathy, the connection, the inner knowing, are all setting off alarms in my head telling me something's up, so what is it?"

They look at each other in silence.

Aeden bites his bottom lip, and Aesher stares off at the ceiling, looking at absolutely nothing, and it's annoying, very annoying.

"What the hell, you guys? What's going on?"

"Aeden, you tell her," Aesher says, finally returning his gaze to the table to join the rest of us.

"Okay," Aeden begins. "First off, sis, we love you, and we are a team, always a team, always have been and always will be."

"I know that. Get to the point." I say, still irritated.

"Well, you know how Aeden and I always dreamed of making it big? And we've gone to several auditions, trying to upsell this twin gig, hoping for a shot?"

"Yes, it's all you guys ever talk about," I say, rolling my eyes.

"Well, we finally got one," he says with a glimmer in his eyes.

"Omg, how amazing! I'm so proud of you guys."

I jump up and run over to hug my brother. I am so excited to get some good news finally, some normal news, something mundane and regular.

"I don't get it. Then why were you guys acting like you were going to drop this horrible bomb on me? I thought we were falling behind on bills or something, and you guys were afraid to tell me."

I add a touch of drama by pretending to wipe the sweat from my forehead.

"Well, that's not all, Ella," Aesher says.

My stomach sinks.

Here it comes, the bomb.

"Aeden and I have to move, and pretty fast too."

"See, the job we got is for that live competition show, Bixie's Drag Battle, and it's already in progress. It just so happens that two of the models quit, and we were on the list as backups; dumb luck, really."

"Hold on, there's no freaking way you guys are drag queens? If that's the case, I'm completely oblivious to life right now. I mean, I support it totally, but..."

Aeden looks to Aesher and starts chuckling, "No, we are not drag queens. We just put in an application to be presenters, to help with the competitions. We had a few auditions, and they put us on their callback list, and now here we are."

"Presenters? Do you mean those practically naked men walking around on stage?"

"That would be us," Aesher answers, while avoiding eye contact once again.

"Well, hey, it's a start, right? A pretty damn good one, if you ask me. Who knows where this opportunity might lead? I haven't watched the show much, but I know Bixie's Drag Battle is pretty big now and only expanding more and more."

"Exactly our thoughts on it," Aeden exclaims, now having a noticeably more genuine smile painted across his face.

While his mood is lightening from having shared their plans with me, mine is dimming with worry because suddenly, I remember the opening of this conversation.

They're moving, which leaves me very few options because there is no way I can afford a three-bedroom apartment alone, working at a furniture store.

I begin to get angry; I know it's selfish, but I can't help it.

"So, what about me, you guys? How am I supposed to find a place so quickly with no warning? Don't you think you should've maybe included me in your plans?"

Aesher strokes his forehead, obviously feeling bad. He's always been super emotional, and I can tell Aeden is picking up on the guilt welling up in him as well, so he spearheads the rest of this family meeting.

"Well, we didn't think by any chance we would get this gig, but once we did, we figured we could still pay for next month, which gives you some time to figure some things out, and worst-case scenario, you can move back in with mom until you find a more permanent plan."

The tears are welling up, and a few escape, no matter how hard I try to hold them back.

They are throwing me away.

"I can't go back. Mom just doesn't get me! She'll label me as a failure and rub your newly found success all in my face, and you know it!"

"She never believed in my dreams, never looked at a single one of my designs, and thought that my love for fashion was a waste of time..."

"...but beloved Aeden and Aesher's dreams to make it on the big screen were all she ever talked about. How could you guys do this to me? I swear you'd be better off as twins. Me, I'm always the afterthought!"

"Aella, it's not like that at all, you know that."

Aeden stands up and attempts to make his way towards me, but I avoid him and dash to my bedroom, wiping tears away, no longer wanting to give them the feeling of satisfaction of hurting me, Aella, the sister of the twins.

I slam my door, sink down behind it, and slow my breathing to a calmer pace, trying to collect myself. There's too much going on, too much to think about.

I need a distraction.

I get up, grab my tablet, and scroll through my tie designs, the ugly polka dots, the over-the-top color splatters, and the lovely safety pins.

None of them are good enough.

I toss my tablet on my bed and head to my closet where all my ties are hanging and rummage through them, the memories fluttering through my mind of when I wore each one, the ones that were gifted or the ones I've purchased, even the ones I've made.

It makes me even sadder because the real reason I even started wearing these ties and wanting to start a collection is because of my brothers.

A nod to being different, the girl from a set of triplets, the girl with two identical brothers, all three with red hair, I thought we were unique, meant to go on this life journey together, always having each other's back, but no, they'd rather be twins.

There's no three of us, just two of them, then me.

I noticed something tucked away in the back of my closet from the corner of my eye, and I forgot I even had it.

I pull it off my shelf.

The dreaded attempted skirt pattern, the one time I tried to sew something different.

I pull it down and fashion it around my waist. It still fits, kind of, but needs a little altering.

Nevertheless, it's what I need right now to clear my head, a passion project that doesn't remind me of any of this crap, no reminders of magic, or my brothers, just something for me.

That's when it hits me.

It's my rebirth. No more Aella, Aeden, and Aesher.

Just me, Aella.

Actually, no, a rebirth is a rebirth.

Fuck the A.

Just me, Ella.

I throw the skirt pattern on my bed, grab a few of my ties off the rack, and get my old-school sewing kit. I'll finalize the design later and do some heavier stitching on the machine when I have more time, but I just want to get this idea out of my head for now.

I begin attaching the ties to the skirt pattern as I think about how I'll reinvent myself, the new me, the just me.

As time passes, the skirt is looking cuter than I expected, and it's definitely unique. If I don't finish anything, I must finish this.

I know Lexie will just absolutely die when she sees it. She's quite the fashionista herself.

I can't believe these bastards haven't even checked on me, not even a knock on the door. Your sister runs off crying, and all you're concerned about is your big TV debut.

The anger is rising in me again, and as the speed of my sewing picks up, it's not long before I prick my finger with the point of the needle.

I feel a sharp sting and see a tiny drop of blood bubble up on my index finger.

I quickly move it to my lips in an attempt to ease the pain.

Suddenly, my body seizes, my hearing dulls, and my vision goes completely white.

Omg, what is happening?!

I try to scream out, but I can't move.

I can't speak.

Slowly, the colors start to trickle back in, and like static fading in and out on the radio between channels, the sound adjusts.

As the figure becomes clear and the objects in the room take their shape, I realize who I'm looking at instantly. Of course, it's him.

It's Yohan.

He's up against the wall.

He looks like he's being choked, but no one's there with their hands around his neck.

It's like a force.

I don't understand it.

He's visibly afraid with his eyes closed shut as he's lifted from the ground.

I'm trying to tune into what he's saying, but it's inaudible.

I try to scream that I'm here. I try to remember the words from the wishing spell, but it's as If I can't interfere.

I can only watch. It's so hard to witness. I want to help him. We're a team.

YOHHAAN!!!

A flash of white overtakes my vision once again, and I slide off my bed and drop to the floor, gasping for air desperately, trying to make sense of what just happened.

I think I just had my first vision, and it's not what I imagined.

Yohan is in trouble, and I hope we still have time.

Don't worry, Yohan, I won't abandon you like my brothers are abandoning me.

You, Lexie, and I are a trio that will last.

One that is genuinely fated.

I don't know how she's doing it, but my first thought is that this must be Madison.

Enough is enough.

I'm done playing games; she's got to go down.

CHAPTER TEN

Yohan

♫ ♫ ♫ *Are you just going to take this? STAND UP. So tired of the fakeness. WAKE UP.* ♫ ♫ ♫

♫ ♫ ♫ *No, we're not going to take it! GET UP.* ♫ ♫ ♫

♫ ♫ ♫ *It's time to GET UP! It's time to STAND UP!* ♫ ♫ ♫

God, I need to change that alarm. It's becoming highly annoying, especially this early in the morning.

I reach for my Cannapuffy and take a few drags while mentally listing what I need to accomplish for the day. I've already decided I'm devoting my day off to looking deeper into this magical mess we've gotten ourselves into, but I'm just not sure exactly where to start.

Maybe the message boards?

Can't Hurt.

I highly doubt I'll be able to find Zeus again because running into him was a coincidence in the first place, and I can't even really recall which online platform I found him on to begin with.

It could've been MagicallyMe, or no, wait, MasterManifestors?

Screw It, I'll try both.

I reach for my laptop and start scrolling through the message boards of MagicallyMe first to see if anything catches my eye, anything mentioning Aiden's Spiral or pages from the Book of Ascension.

Nothing, but all hope is not lost just yet. I'm just starting out, after all.

I choose to minimize the page and open a new browser for Master-Manifestors.

This one requires a login, which seems hopeful because that means I most likely would've spent more time on here if I chose to sign up and go through that whole process.

Now if I could just remember the damn username and password.

I take another hit from my puffy and try to think...

It would've probably been something stupid knowing me, something with a combination of my name...

I've signed up for so many random sites through the years that it could literally be anything.

I try combos I might have used.

MagicYoYo33... Nope.

YohanManifests86... Negative.

YoMagicHan... Access Denied.

The password's not the issue, and I know it because even though it's not the smartest thing concerning web-based activity, I usually try to use similar versions of my base password to make access just a bit easier.

You would think they would have a forgot password button, but nope, you lose your login info, and you're screwed, but I guess that's to add to the mysticism of it all.

I stare off at the wall at one of my paintings I have hanging while I try to pick my brain a little bit more. It's too early to give up, and with this Madison character targeting us, we need to figure this all out sooner rather than later.

The painting reminds me of Bash, who I still haven't heard from in a few days. I avoided going on V-Messenger just because I didn't want to be disappointed and find him still offline.

A part of me feels like maybe he's avoiding me, and that's okay, right?

The truth is, people grow apart from each other, and maybe he needs to be around more people who can offer him better advice than I can.

I feel like I'm always looking to him for help, and it's one-sided and unfair.

He deserves better.

A personality like his is meant to shine and inspire.

He's full of color, personality, and vibrancy, and that belongs on display, not hidden from the world.

I'm an idiot.

That's when it hits me: color, Bash, the influence for my username around that time.

ColorMagick33.

I type in my username and password and explore the interface.

In an instant, it all comes rushing back to me, my minor obsession with trying to find out the secrets to life and trying to influence my life for the better.

I scroll through threads, looking for the same key terms: The book of Ascension, magical pages, ambiguous emails, just anything that will point me in the right direction.

Of course, there is a lack of information to be found, and just when I think I hit another wall, a message pops up.

HeyZeuz99: Long time, bro. Where the heck have you been?

ColorMagick33: Wow, Zeus! Bro, I didn't think I'd be able to find you again. Me, the usual. Moving kind of fell off the scene.

HeyZeuz99: Ah, I see. Well, I'm happy you're back. So, did you find it?

ColorMagick33: Find what?

HeyZeuz99: What you were looking for, of course. Everyone comes here looking for something, but I think I just answered my own question because if you found it, you wouldn't be back, now, would you?

ColorMagick33: Zeus, please stop riddling me right now. I actually need your help. Do you remember that book you told me about? That Book of Ascension?

HeyZeuz99: But of course, I willed Aiden's Spiral to you as a start. How could I forget?

ColorMagick33: You willed It to me? This is happening because of what you did?

HeyZeuz99: Of course not. I am not the source. This is happening because it's meant to. It's fated—your destiny. Written in the stars or however you'd like to word it.

ColorMagick33: Well, how do I get more pages? Can you will them to me? I really need help, this girl. She's after me and my friends, and I think she's legit.

HeyZeuz99: Sorry, I can't do that—the pages they choose you. I've done all I can. All I was meant to.

ColorMagick33: You literally just said you can will shit to me! Now I was chosen by pages in a book? Make it make sense, Zeus! Why even bother messaging me?

HeyZeus99: I messaged you because I know you came here to find me, and what's the harm in catching up with an old friend? I willed you the spiral because I was meant to. I told you, you will find the answers. You have to trust in that.

ColorMagick33: Trust in the fact that the answers will come flying in out of nowhere when this crazy she-devil Madison is hell-bent on making my life a living hell? I need more than that.

HeyZeus99: Wait? Madison? It wouldn't be this Madison, would it?

A photo of Madison pops up in my chat box, and my stomach turns. The blonde hair, that evil little smile. I really dislike this girl.

ColorMagick33: Yes, her! Who is she? How do you know her?

HeyZeus99: She's bad news. I suggest you master the spiral if you haven't done so already. You were right. She's definitely coming after you. She's power-hungry, and I would...

My computer freezes, and my chat box scrolls back up to exactly where the picture of Madison is still lingering.

The photo glides out of the chat box, expands, and the image changes before my eyes into the version of Madison I encountered the other night, but more recent and now animated.

"Hello bitches, you having fun discussing yours truly?"

She offers up her vomit-inducing wide grin to us via webcam.

Not again.

"What do you want, Madison?" I ask, trying to keep my tone as neutral as possible.

"The pages, duh! I thought I was clear, Hun, but I guess not, so yeah, the pages, I want the pages, and please stop discussing me with your little friend here..."

"...like Zeus of all people, is who you choose to ask for help? Ha-ha, you're better off spending your time trying to convince Lexie to will me the pages."

"Oh yeah, and by the way, I told you I'm a tech witch, honey. It doesn't take a genius to figure out that online resources are probably not your best bet."

"Don't be fooled by the pink ensemble, trinkets, and tchotchkes. I might be cute, but I will still absolutely ruin you."

"I'm not afraid of you, Madison. We're going to..."

"I'll stop you there. You are clearly afraid or wouldn't be desperately searching for an answer throughout these message boards..."

"...and Zeus, babes, I know you're just playing spectator in this conversation right now, but before I have to log you out of everything permanently... I suggest you stop feeding Yo-Yo here information."

"He's my toy, not yours."

All the windows on my screen close, except for Madison's stream, unfortunately.

"The pages, I need the pages, so let's get those to me ASAP before I have to resort to... other tactics."

She plays with her nails while staring at the camera. I assume she is waiting for a response, but I have nothing to say.

She continues.

"Okay, Yo-Yo, I'll leave you to it, but realize the time is ticking by, and the more time it takes, the angrier I'll get, and this, this is me calm, so let's not escalate this further, ok?"

"Oh, and one last thing, you might want to sign into your V-Messenger. I think you have something waiting for you."

"One of your little boyfriends, I think. Ha-ha, Love Ya. Muah."

She blows an unwanted kiss, and her video stream disappears.

I take a minute to try to process everything that just happened, but it isn't long before my mind switches focus.

Oh my God... Bash.

She better not have done anything to Bash.

I quickly pull up V-Messenger, but as I'm about to log in, I hear a heavy knock at my door.

I close my laptop and make my way to the door, questioning who it could possibly be.

Lexie and Ella haven't been to my apartment yet, so I doubt they know where I even live, and besides that, how would they get past the main entrance without me letting them in?

My dad has a key, obviously, and he isn't very social, so I haven't seen him bring any friends over or anything, unless maybe when I'm at work.

Knock Knock

"I'm coming, I'm coming. Give me a second."

God, whoever is knocking is banging the damn door like they own the place. Whatever happened to being subtle? Does that not exist anymore?

I twist the door handle and pull it open slightly because if this is an in-person visit from Madison, I'm totally slamming the door in her face.

It's not Madison.

It's Him.

It's Nash.

"Hey, Yohan, So I know it's early, and I hope this isn't weird or anything, but I figured we live in the same building, so it wouldn't hurt to stop by and maybe talk about those designs."

"I mean, if you're free, that is. If not, I can totally come back."

His eyes.

His eyes are glossy and inviting. There's an innocence behind them that's calling to me, a kindness that I want to be on the receiving end of.

I'm lost in them, completely lost.

"Yohan?"

Shit, I'm doing it again.

"Yeah, sorry, just waking up, you know, still adjusting, but yeah, no, I'm free. Did you want to come in, or if you give me a second, I can change really quick, and we can head out?"

He smiles, and God, that smile.

"We can hang here if you don't mind, and I won't soak up all your time, I promise."

He winks at me, and I grow warm.

I can do this. I can do this.

"Totally, I mean come in."

He makes his way into my apartment, and I try not to be awkward in the best ways I can, being aware of my mannerisms and keeping my eyes to myself no matter how bad they are dying to explore him.

"Ah, your apartment is pretty cool. Is that one of your art pieces you were telling me about?" he says, pointing to a painted portrait of a random lady sitting at a bar.

"Ha-ha, no, that's my dad's. My style's a little... different."

He chuckles and takes a seat on my sofa.

"Well, when do I get the pleasure of seeing said artwork?" he says, grinning again, and my insides are going crazy.

If it's butterflies, there's a hell of a lot of them, and they are having a freaking field day in my stomach right now.

I quickly reply.

"Uh, I can show you a few things now. Let me just grab my sketch-book from my room. It'll only take a second."

"No rush."

I make my way to my room, trying not to stumble or make myself look stupid in any way because that's just something I would do.

As soon as I get to my room, I let out a long breath of relief.

Yohan, he's a human being, just like you. Get it together. You got this.

I look around my room for my sketchbook and quickly find it under the t-shirt I threw off when I got in last night, a little hungover from all the whiskey shots and head spinning from the séance.

That's when I realize.

I'm shirtless. Crap.

I grab that same t-shirt, hit it with just a hint of body spray, and return to my living room, where Nash is sitting and smiling at me once again.

Stop seducing me, you bastard.

"Got it," I say with a half-smile, holding my sketchbook slightly in the air.

Do I sit next to him? Should I stand?

Help.

I hand him my sketchbook and take a seat next to him, being sure to leave a decent gap of space between us.

I'm nervous.

My sketches are the goth fantasy type, and I don't want him to think I'm weird and sit here daydreaming about mystical creatures all day and living in a fantasy land.

I just like to draw them.

It's my outlet.

I'm curiously studying his reactions to my drawings, and it looks like it's going in a positive direction.

Thank God.

"Whoa, Yohan, this is better than I even thought. How do you come up with this stuff? The detail is crazy good! Like I could see this actually existing, like actually being real."

He holds up my sketchbook and shows me the page with my sketch of what I would describe as a salamander, but with wings.

I call him Garth.

"Thanks, I appreciate it," I say, hiccupping on my words.

He goes silent, and his eyes return to my sketchbook, flipping through pages, scanning my artwork, and grinning at my designs.

I can't help but take the time to steal glances at him here and there.

While he's stuck on a page of one of my dragons, I focus my gaze on his lips.

They're so perfect, slightly thin, but not any less bewitching, calling me in, and I want to answer.

I want to answer that call so badly.

Yohan. Stop.

I'm realistic, so I'm pretty sure a guy this charming and good-looking probably won't find a guy like me attractive, and I'm pretty sure he's straight anyway, but being friends couldn't hurt, right?

I'm sure the attraction would wear off once he starts talking about the girls he's interested in, or even the girlfriend he probably already has.

"You alright over there, Yohan? You're so quiet." He says, now looking at me again.

I break free from all the overthinking I just subjected myself to and attempt to make conversation.

"Yeah, I'm good. Sorry, I was just thinking about work, you know, new job and all, information overload."

"Totally get it."

"So, I love your stuff, dude. Are you still down to design something for me? It would be awesome to sport one of your pieces. I know no one will have anything like it, and it will be unique."

"Yeah, I can do that. Anything particular in mind?"

He looks up at my ceiling and then back at me.

"I think I want it to be artist's choice. You're hella creative, from what I see. Maybe you can make something up for me."

"I'm down," I say, and I'm sure I'm turning red. An attractive guy not only loves my artwork, but also complimented me.

So much for ruining my day, Madison. I'm on cloud nine right now, ha ha. Talk about ascension.

"Thanks." He says and places his hand on my knee.

I jump up so fast without even realizing it, and now I'm sure I'm red, probably freaking crimson.

"Shit, sorry dude, I didn't mean to be offensive or anything, I just..."

I stutter out a response.

"N-no, no, it's ok. I just get a little anxious sometimes."

"Okay, noted. No touching Yohan, ha-ha."

No, not what I meant. You can touch Yohan.

Actually, please do...

"Well, I hope this doesn't change things. You'll still make that piece for me, right?"

"Of course."

"Awesome, well, Yohan, it was cool getting to see your art. I'll stop by later in the week and check in if that's ok?"

"Yes, I should have something, at least a starter sketch, by the weekend, if that's cool."

"That's perfect," he says as he approaches the door.

I unlock the door for him, and as he's making his way out, he pauses for a second, and we lock eyes. I feel like everything in the world stops, and the air tightens between us.

"I really appreciate it. You know you're a cool guy."

And you, you're so... everything...

"You too, uh, see you on the weekend?"

"Ha-ha, see you on the weekend." He turns and makes his way down the hall.

I leave the door open for a moment to watch him walk away.

My dream guy walking away.

I make my way back to my room, still drunk with desire and longing from my brief interaction with Nash.

I lay on my bed, getting lost in a daydream about what could possibly happen between us if something ever did.

How he would be the perfect guy for me. I know I barely know him, but it's something I can just feel.

I'm sure I'm not the only one who has experienced feelings like this before. I'm pretty sure they say love at first sight is a thing, and this is sighting number two.

His eyes, His lips, that voice.

That calm, soothing voice.

I roll to my side and clench my pillow, swooning and craving, but it's not long before I spot my laptop and remember.

Bash!

I quickly hop out of bed, sit at my desk, and prop open my laptop.

I sign into V-Messenger, and Bash is still offline, but I notice there is a video message waiting for me, and it's from him.

I notice he's back in his makeup, and it makes me feel a little bit better because I know he's not feeling as down about himself as he was when we last talked, and he's back to sporting his authenticity.

I quickly click play, and the video begins to stream.

He's whispering and sounds scared.

What a minute ago was a sense of relief has shifted to a feeling of concern.

"Yohan, I hate to do this to you, but I don't know who else to turn to. There's something weird going on here..."

He keeps looking behind him, visibly fearful that someone might hear him.

"I only did it because I wanted to be around people like me, but now I need help. They keep talking about magic or witchcraft or something. I want to leave, but they won't let me..."

I am going to kill Madison.

"... he's not the person they think he is. They're talking about harvesting energy. It's so weird. I don't know, Yohan, Help, I'm so scared. I don't know what you can do or if you can do anything but—"

A figure appears behind him, and his voice joins the audio.

"I told you, you can't be on your phone. It's part of the contract you signed. No leaks whatsoever. Now get back to..."

The video stops.

What the hell is this? Where is he?

I zoom into the frame where the video has ended to see if I can make out the figure talking to him.

The frame is pixelated, but there's one thing I notice.

It's another boy like him.

Another boy in makeup.

Chapter Eleven

Lexie

*I*NHALE FOR 5, HOLD *for 3, exhale slowly.*

"As you inhale, picture a bright white light entering through the top of your head and making its way through your body, cleansing all worry, releasing all tension."

Inhale for 5, hold for 3, exhale slowly.

"As you exhale, picture that light carrying all these negative thoughts and emotions and releasing them back down into the earth from the soles of your feet."

Inhale for 5, hold for 3, exhale slowly.

"As you connect with the energy of the earth, remember, all energy is equal. You too are..."

Oh, screw it.

I have too much on my mind for this right now.

I hit pause on my meditation and check the time on my phone.

I still have some time to kill before work, so I reach for Ms. Cookie Dough and take a generous swig from the bottle.

As I'm getting ready and mentally prepping myself for this long day ahead of me, which will be more than daunting seeing as how both Yohan and Ella have the day off, I hear my sister's footsteps hurrying off to her room, followed by the quiet click of her door.

I have to admit; I have been feeling a little bit guilty that I haven't been spending as much time with her ever since all of this quote-un-quote magic crap showed up in my life, but I'm sure she knows I'm still here if she needs me.

That's what sisters are for, right?

Either way, with time to spare, I decide to check on her, give her a little impromptu visit from her big sis, and maybe schedule a fun night for us. I'm sure I can figure out a way to carve out some time. I know she looks up to me, and it's essential that I maintain that.

I carefully make my way down the hall, ensuring my footsteps are light. I think she is way overdue for a jump scare, and I want to execute it well.

When I make it to her door, I lean closer and listen in, waiting for the right moment to burst in and pay my surprise visit.

See, Xyla, you're not the only one who can play detective.

I hear her bumbling around like she's searching for something, and a familiar scent comes wafting from underneath the door.

Incense?

Since when is she into that stuff?

Her footsteps come to a halt; she grows silent, and I hear several clicks of what sounds like a lighter.

Oh, hell no!

I continue to listen, calm myself down for a second, and rationalize before I make my way in.

The last thing I want to do is barge in there angry and destroy her trust in me.

I want to have a calm approach while discussing whatever she is doing to appear firm but practical.

The clicking stops.

"M-Maya O Odin Release, Maya O Odin R-Release."

The eff.

The calm approach is no longer an option.

I reach for the door handle, quickly make my way into her room, and close the door.

"Xyla, what the heck are you doing?!?"

"N-Nothing."

She blows out the candle in front of her quickly, throws her doll Kenzie to the side, and stands up, meeting my eyes for a second before quickly hanging her head down and focusing her gaze on the floor.

"Xyla, I'm serious!"

She looks back up at me; her face displaying a look of guilt as she begins her explanation.

"I'm sorry, Lex. I just wanted to help. I saw you guys the other night. I was watching. I don't want Madison to hurt you. We're sisters, were supposed to protect each other."

I feel my heart sink, and I try to put my anger to the side.

I know she just wanted to spend time with me, and she was probably just genuinely curious about what me and my friends were doing.

Can I blame her? I was that age once.

"Listen Xy, this stuff you saw, it's not a game, ok? It's scary, and I don't want you messing around with it. The last thing I need is you getting hurt while I figure all of this out."

"But I can help. I'm good at piecing things together and investigating. I can help get Madison to leave you alone."

"Listen…" I bend down to meet her at eye level.

"… you are an amazing detective, but you're only eleven. This is your time for fun. Trust me, when you get older like me, you'll have your own set of problems to tackle and things to investigate. For now, just be a kid. You'll thank me later…"

"… besides, you know your sis is a boss. Madison is the least of my worries, okay, girl?"

She giggles. "Okay, I'm sorry, Lex."

"It's okay, but don't mention any of this to mom and dad, OK? If they find out either of us did any of this, we're both in for it."

She makes a motion, pretending to lock her lips with an imaginary key and throws it over her shoulders.

"Alright, Xyla, I'm heading to work. Movie night later?"

"Yay, a new movie about psychic investigators just came out. I was waiting to watch it with you."

"Sounds perfect. See ya after work."

I grab the candle and incense from the floor and exit her room, shutting the door quietly.

What the hell?

As if there aren't enough things to deal with, my sister is over here trying to recreate the séance I'm now wishing I never did.

I need a vacation.

I head to my room, finish getting ready, and make my way to the Furnish, aka the *Torture Chamber*.

As soon as I walk through the doors of the building, I instantly wish I was smart enough to call out today. I could've come up with something, anything at all, to avoid this day that I know is going to take forever to get through.

I walk through the departments leading to mine, and on my way, I run into none other than brown-nosing Jaden, whose energy is high-level and perkier than usual.

"Hey Lexie, love the hairstyle today."

I'd love it if you just pretended I didn't exist today.

"Hey, Jaden, how are you?"

"Good, good. Are you excited about the meeting later? I heard there are some significant changes coming. Maybe it'll be something beneficial for us."

I try to keep my facial expressions under control, but in my mind, I am so annoyed at how much he loves it here.

"I am ecstatic, Jaden. The only adjective I can use to describe my feelings towards this meeting is nothing than utterly ecstatic."

He rolls into laughter. "Oh, Lexie, you are too funny."

"Well, I'll see you there!" he exclaims as he continues to walk to wherever he is heading.

"See you there," I mimic as I continue my journey to Home Offices, where the customers/masochists await to ruin my life.

When I finally get to my station, I place my bag on the counter and sign in.

"Excuse me, miss, I was wondering..." a voice from behind me begins to ask.

"We don't have any more lime green binders!" I say as I turn to face him.

God, where did that outburst come from?

Get it together, Lex.

"Umm, yeah, I know. I'm actually here with a couple of cases. I just need a signature."

I reach for the clipboard, compare the boxes to the listed quantity, and transcribe my signature, feeling guilty that I just gave this guy my attitude.

He's just doing his job.

"I'm sorry, it's just been a long day you wouldn't even believe..."

He cuts me off.

"Don't care, just dropping these off."

He takes the clipboard back with what feels like a snatch and keeps it moving.

You see, this is why. This is why I cannot do this anymore. Even the damn delivery guy has an attitude. I can't.

I need a new job.

Aside from my little run-in with the delivery guy, the rest of my social interactions were reasonably decent. I spend time organizing the department and helping customers locate items while I wait for my turn to attend the company meeting.

Gianni, our store manager, suggested we try something new and have smaller meetings in batches while the free coworkers covered the departments in need, which I don't mind.

The fewer people to interact with, the better.

When it's finally my time to go in, I notice Rose and Jaden making their way to the onboarding room where the meeting is being held.

Ugh, couldn't they have been in another group?

I mean, there are at least fifty people on shift right now.

I follow behind them while scrolling through my phone, praying they don't turn around and attempt to have a conversation with me.

It looks like I am in luck because they make their way in, and I follow suit unnoticed.

When I make my way into the room, I carefully choose a seat in the back and slouch down, hoping this goes by quickly. I mean, there can't be that much to go over.

There never is.

Gianni begins the meeting by reminding us to sign in, do our monthly security training, and gives a quick overview of the break policy updates.

He then continues to remind us of all the things we already know.

"Remember, working here at FURNISH, we pride ourselves on making the customer our utmost priority. I expect to see all employees following the guidelines and giving customers their full attention, which means no phone usage on the sales floor, with the exception of emergencies."

I roll my eyes and quickly rub them to mask my annoyance.

He continues.

"That being said, I would like to announce a few changes happening that I'm sure will help with productivity and increase overall team morale."

"First thing first, I would like to congratulate Jaden. He has recently been promoted to floor manager and will be overseeing Bedrooms, Home Offices, and Kitchens. Jaden has been a prime example of what we here at Furnish expect from our employees by being reliable, knowledgeable, and always willing to help. I would like to thank you, Jaden, for your ongoing dedication, and we look forward to the talent you bring with you as lead."

The room begins to clap enthusiastically, and I do my best to imitate their ardor, although I'm unsure if I'm actually successful.

"So, moving along, thank you again, Jaden. We have had some complaints from a few coworkers lately regarding the workload in each department..."

Oh God, here we go.

"… so we have come up with a solution. Starting next week, our departments will begin going on rotation. You will be cross-trained in two additional departments led by your current manager. We hope that this change will help eradicate any further…."

buzz

♫ ♫ ♫ *Girl, shake that ass if you a hoe, don't be scared, girl, twerk and let um know* ♫ ♫ ♫

buzz

♫ ♫ ♫ Don't be afraid to let it show. Release the hoe, release the hoe… ♫ ♫ ♫

I reach into my pocket, hoping no one notices, and try to press my volume rocker down to kill the noise.

MADISON!

The room goes silent, and I feel my skin flush immediately.

My phone continues to buzz in my pocket incessantly, but now, thankfully, without audio.

"Okay, completely inappropriate. I hope whoever's phone that was is now on silent, but as I was saying…"

Gianni continues to go through the points of the meeting, which to me now are entirely irrelevant.

All I can think about is Madison and how I am going to destroy her when I finally get my hands on her.

As the meeting comes to an end, I quickly make my way to the coworker bathroom, the one no one ever uses, where there is only one stall, and I know I can talk freely.

My phone has been vibrating nonstop in my pocket ever since she decided to thoroughly embarrass me in front of everyone, and I cannot wait to answer and give her a piece of my mind.

I enter the bathroom, lock the door, and take my phone out of my pocket.

There is no button to answer the call. She is already there.

Creepy

"I am going to kill you!"

She laughs, "You would have to find me first, Hun. Ha-ha, what's wrong? Are you upset I revealed your true identity to your coworkers? I mean, it's not a secret love. I'm sure they already knew of your salacious nature..."

"...besides, I did you a favor. You know I could've just turned the volume right back up, right? Ha-ha,"

I feel the anger building up in me, and she is so lucky, so lucky that she hides behind a screen all the time.

"I don't get your little obsession with me, Madison. I'm not giving you the pages, and your basic ass tricks don't scare me."

She raises an eyebrow at the screen.

"Girl, you are nothing to be obsessed with. I just like collecting things, and you have something that belongs in my collection."

"Also, if you're going to be a witch, obviously a basic one, but that's beside the point. You should learn the correct terms."

"I need you to will them to me, not give them to me."

She giggles.

"I'm not willing you shit. Like I said before, not a damn thing. You are wasting your time."

There it goes, that little evil glare, that little shift in her personality that trademarks her as a psychopath.

She grits her teeth.

"Well, you do remember what the second option was, don't you?"

She leans in closer to the camera.

"Is that a threat, Madison? Are you threatening to kill me?

"Am I?" she responds as she begins to file her nails.

"I wouldn't threaten me if I were you."

The nail filing stops.

"I just did, bitch."

She disappears from my screen, and I'm left alone in the bathroom, head spinning with thoughts of how I will solve this, any of this.

I try to shake away the annoyance and anger that has built up inside me within the last half an hour and attempt to put my phone back in my pocket, but before I can, a message from the Haus of Ascension grouper pops up on my phone.

Haus of Ascension

Aella

Hey, our usual spot tonight after you get out of work, Lexie?

Yohan, I know you're off. Hopefully, you'll be free. I have to tell you guys something.

I don't trust text, evil psycho tech bitch on the loose in the environment.

P.S. I hope you read that part, Madison. I know you're stalking our texts.

Yohan

I'll be there.

I'm in.

P.S. Fuck You Madison. *heart emoji*

The rest of the day goes by surprisingly quickly. Maybe because I'm lost in my thoughts, my thoughts about Madison, what happened with my sister, and what more Ella could possibly add to the mountain of problems we are already facing?

After work, I head home, take a quick shower, and change into something cute to lighten my mood.

If I'm going out, I am going out looking good.

I catch a Dryve to Eat Your Heart Out Bakery and make my way to our usual table, which, for some reason, is always empty, and empty it is.

I am the first one there.

I notice Yohan from the corner of my eye entering the doorway and signal him over.

He's in surprisingly good spirits.

Usually, it's hard to gauge his mood by his disposition, but today, it's clear he's had a good day.

A day off can do that for you.

"Hey, Lexie," he says, as he grabs a seat at our table.

"What's up, Mr. Yo-Yo? You seem all cheery and upbeat."

"Oh, nothing, just good to have a day to myself, you know." He responds, blushing, and it's so obvious he's keeping something to himself.

"Should we wait for Ella to order drinks, or..." Before he can finish his sentence, I am instantly distracted by her.

Ella.

I notice her slide through the door of Eat Your Heart Out Bakery, and she is serving.

Who is this girl?

She struts through the aisle of tables, and I try to take in her new look.

It's so different from what I'm used to, but it's so her.

Really her.

Her gorgeous red hair is tied into two buns held together by chopsticks adorned with cute little bows at the end.

Her lipstick, a popping glossy red.

Her top is a simple button-up tied above her belly button, revealing not too much but just enough; it's a statement.

But the thing that catches my eye the most, the most unique thing about this entire ensemble that she is wearing the hell out of right now, is the skirt.

The skirt is stunning.

I watch as she makes her way to the table and the assortment of ties that are pieced together to make this skirt sway gracefully as she walks.

I recognize most of them: some I've gifted, some she's bought, some she's made.

It's a skirt made of memories, and it is extraordinary.

"Hey guys," she says casually as she grabs a seat at the table.

"Hey," Yohan responds, and I can see the awe in his eyes as well, clearly as stunned by Ella's fashion statement as I am.

"Who is she, though?" I say as I eye her up and down and offer up my smile of approval.

She adjusts one of the chopsticks in her hair.

"Oh, her?"

She adjusts her top.

"She's Ella."

"Ella without the A."

(A) Ella

"Lexie, please tell me you brought your hairbrush."

"Girl, you know I don't go anywhere without it, but what has gotten into you?" she says as she hands me her hairbrush flask.

I unscrew the bottom and take a massive gulp of whiskey, not really caring who is watching me at this point.

I have way more significant problems.

"No time for that phones off, and let's get to it."

I take my phone out of my pocket and power it off because who knows what tricks Madison has up her sleeves, and I do not plan on giving her a leg up by allowing her to eavesdrop as we plan her downfall.

I watch Lexie and Yohan power off their phones while looking at me quizzically.

I guess they are not used to this side of me, but neither am I, but I do know one thing: I like it.

This is me. The real me.

"All right, now that we can talk freely, let's get down to it. I say it's time we vanquish this bitch once and for all!"

"Okay, have you been binge-watching 90s witch sitcoms again? I'm just asking because, in case you didn't notice, I think we're a little more basic here. I don't think any of us are going to be moving things with our minds, seeing the future, or freezing time anytime soon." Lexie says with a chuckle.

"Well, for your information, one of those three things has already happened. It's why I wanted to talk to you guys, actually."

"Wait, what, which one?" Yohan asks, now leaning forward, obviously interested.

"My wish came true. I had a vision, and it wasn't good, and now that I think about it, it was actually scary, no, horrifying, the experience was horrifying."

"Can I get you guys anything to drink for starters, maybe an appetizer?" our waitress asks.

I didn't even notice her there; it's like she pops up out of nowhere, and it's always her, Patra.

"Three Bloodbath's please," Yohan answers quickly. I assume to get rid of her so we can move this conversation along.

Patra writes down our orders and heads away from the table to get our drinks, so I continue my spiel.

"Yeah, it's hard to explain. I was just working on my skirt, and all of a sudden, my vision went white, then came back, and I was watching you, Yohan."

I see his face tighten with worry.

"Of course, it's me, always me. Any more whiskey left in that hairbrush, Lex?"

Lexie hands him the hairbrush, and I continue to explain.

"It was so weird, but I think it's Madison. I saw you like being choked or something, but no one was there. It was like a force, but no figure, no anything."

"That's creepy as all hell," Lexie adds as Patra places our drinks on the table.

I take a large sip from my Bloodbath, and I feel the buzz from the liquor hit me instantly.

God, I needed this.

I needed this so much.

"Well, I'm not surprised. I tried reaching out to Zeus, you know, to get some information, which wasn't very helpful, but in the process, Madison basically hijacked both of our screens and, you know, made her threats like she does."

"Omg, speaking of outlandish Madison's antics, let me tell you!" Lexie exclaims, followed by a sip of her drink.

"She basically hacked into my phone during my meeting at work earlier and played a song professing that I was a hoe on high volume, and I was so annoyed."

I can't help but burst out laughing. I mean, if it were me, it totally wouldn't be funny, but from a spectator's point of view, hilarious.

"Really, Ella?" she says before finding herself chuckling as well.

"Okay, I know we need to figure this all out, but can we talk about regular stuff for a minute? It's like this magic mess has taken over our whole lives."

She's right. There's plenty of time to plan Madison's demise. Plus, I think we need more information, more magic, more something before we try to execute any type of plan.

"So, Mr. Yo-Yo, what's going on with you? You seem a little happier than usual. I don't even have to use my newly found psychic abilities to tell there's a little shift in your personality over there."

He starts to blush a little and is clearly trying to hide it.

"Oh, come on, spill it," Lexie adds, nudging him in the arm.

"Um, so I kind of met a guy. His name is Nash. It's not like we're talking or dating or anything, but I kind of like him, and it's a good distraction, but I'm sure he's straight, so it doesn't really matter. It's just cool, you know."

"Wait, Nash? Isn't that the friend you said was missing, so you've heard from him?" I ask.

"No, that's Bash, but yeah, I did hear from Bash. It was creepy. I know you said to stray away from the Madison thing, but she told me to check my messenger, and when I did, I found a message from him, like he was being held captive and asking for help."

"What the hell, is nothing off limits for this girl? We have to watch our friends and family, too. I cannot wait to meet this girl. She is in for it." Lexie states while clenching her fists.

"Yeah, I need to figure out where he is. I'm hoping he sends me another video so I can track him down, but right now, I just feel lost in the whole thing, and it sucks because he's depending on me."

"Don't worry, we are going to find him, Yohan, and as for her. We are going to end her."

I feel for him, and it's making me hate Madison even more.

I try to bring the mood back up because I can see he's losing that glow he walked in with. Plus, I want to hear about this mystery guy.

"So, who's this Nash guy?"

There it goes, that smile, that tinge of glow, it's back.

I don't know if it's the liquor in me, but I get so excited for him like I'm the one who's met someone.

I'm just over here living vicariously, I guess.

"Details, Details," I squeal, now edging on my seat.

"Yas Hun, spill the tea," Lexie says, head now fully tilted towards him and resting on her arm.

"Uh, he lives in my apartment complex. He said he likes my tattoos and asked me to do a design for him. I said yes, he's coming over this weekend to see the design."

"Oh yeah, and he touched my knee, and I freaked out like an idiot." He places his face in his palms.

"Omg, he totally likes you," Lexie says while she stirs her drink with her straw.

"Yeah, agreed. He broke the touch barrier early on. That's a thing. I read it in a book once." I say, happy to add my expertise.

He takes his face from his palm, and he's now wearing a noticeable smile. I think he wanted some type of confirmation from an outside view, and we provided it to him.

"I guess we'll have to wait and find out. I'll keep you guys posted, though."

"Please do."

Our waitress, Patra, comes back to the table, and we make our usual order of dessert rolls with the addition of a noodle sampler plate to share.

"What about you, Miss Ella, without the A, What have you been up to? It seems like a little more than magic has gotten to you lately. I know my best friend, honey."

I take yet another colossal sip of my drink, and If I wasn't feeling it before, boy, am I feeling it now.

"It's my freaking brothers, Lexie. They moved out and told me like the night before. They're going to be on that damn drag show, and I want to be happy for them, but what about me? How am I supposed to afford a three-bedroom apartment by myself? I don't want to go back to live with my mother, and I only have a month to figure it all out.”

“Wait a minute, you’re a triplet with identical brothers who are both drag queens?” Yohan asks with the most shocked look on his face.

I couldn’t even recreate his current expression if I tried.

“No, they said they are going to be presenters or something I don’t know.”

“Oh, okay, girl, because I was lost for a minute, too. I’m like Aedan and Aesher drag queens? I know we’ve gone through a lot of unexpected shit in such a short amount of time, but that would be jaw-dropping.”

I laugh, “I know, right? Could you imagine?”

“Well, maybe they’ll end up famous. Bixie’s is a big thing right now, you know,” Lexie adds.

I roll my eyes. “Yeah, I know.”

The drinks are hitting, and the room is doing that thing it does when I’ve had just a bit too much, so I decide to push my cocktail to the side and focus on my noodles.

As I’m munching away on the savory udon that I am so thankful for at the moment, I notice two people walking up to our table.

A guy and a girl.

The guy looks nerdy, with a tight button-up shirt, khaki pants, glasses, and his sandy brown hair neatly groomed.

The girl is the opposite.

She has what I would describe as a Harajuku-type style, very colorful but edgy, a beautiful, tattooed sleeve that looks like it is paying homage to all things under the sea, and diamond dermal piercings decorate the side of her face in the shape of a star.

I stop chewing to take them in as they approach our table.

The girl speaks first.

"You're going to need our help, and before you jump to conclusions, the only reason we're here is because we hate her just as much as you."

Where do I know that voice from?

The guy comments next.

"She's not who you think she is, and she really isn't that powerful. We just need a plan, a good one."

The girl continues.

"Quite frankly, we're tired of being in the background. We have our own stories, too, and we're more than capable of going on the hunt for the pages ourselves."

That's it! Madison's henchmen, the people in the background of that video, Reggie, and...

Before I can even finish my thought process, I hop to my feet in full defense mode because tonight is our night for peace and coming up with a plan. I can't handle more drama.

Not tonight.

"We don't need your help, Reggie and friend! For all we know, she sent you here, and our phones are off. How the hell did you even track us? Never mind that we have enough problems..."

Lexie stands and quickly interrupts.

"Ella, calm down. We need as much help as we can get right now. Let's be honest. We have little to work with at the moment. The more information we have, the better the chance of taking her down."

"Ella, I think Lexie has a point. We need information. I can keep trying my resources, but who knows how far that will get us? Besides, the more people, the better."

They are making sense; I just want this to be over. I want everything to go back to normal.

"Okay, all right, fine, let's at least hear what you guys have to say."

We scoot our seats over at the table so Reggie and his friend can take a seat. She begins to explain, and I can tell she's the real brains behind their whole little magical group.

"So, my name is Quinn, and I help Madison with most of the tech stuff as far as software goes. It's not as magical as she makes it seem. Yes, the magic helps, but without a starting point, you're nowhere. Think of it as any other magical tool, like a crystal, for example. You need to charge that crystal. You need to bring it to life."

"Reggie here. He does the hardware. I've never been interested in that portion of the tech world, so I'm glad to have him on board. Long story short, Madison collects pages, she threatens, she manipulates, and I'm pretty sure she's killed."

"We ended up with her because she made us a deal: we would will each other the pages and work together because she saw technology as a way to reach a broader range of witches, which at the time made a lot of sense to me."

"As time progressed, I started to realize if what they say is accurate, and once all the pages are collected, and we ascend or whatever, and become this afterlife powerhouse...."

"...with a personality like hers, she would want complete power and turn against us."

"I was right. I started going against my morals and using tech magic to monitor her. She's been collecting side pages and making deals without us, and I'm just not going to sit here and wait for her to off me in my sleep. The bitch needs to go, and the time is now."

My head is spinning. That was a lot of information to process, and damn, this girl can talk. She's smart nonetheless, and I have a change of heart.

I want them on our team.

"Another round of drinks?" Creepy Patra comes lurking in to interrupt when it's just all starting to get juicy.

"Sure", Lexie replies.

"A round of Scythe Wielders good?"

"Sure," the table echoes, almost in unison, clearly wanting to return to the conversation.

Patra takes our order and walks to the bar in her usual slithering fashion.

"So, what do we do? Where do we start?" Lexie takes the words right out of my mouth.

Reggie, who has been eerily silent, finally speaks up.

"In all honesty, you guys are already a step ahead. Whatever protection magic you are using is strong. She's tried other things, aside from the annoying little pop-ups on your devices, but nothing worked. You guys have some energy protecting you from the magic on the pages she does have. Whatever it is, keep using it."

The wishing spell.

"But to answer your question, we start by devising a plan. She needs to be taken down in person, somewhere without much tech that she can manipulate, somewhere in nature. She's so focused on using technology that most of what she's collected that we know of lacks the knowledge of the old ways, earth magic. She'll be weakest there."

"Earth magic? There are categories?" Yohan asks.

"Not really, it's all a spectrum, but it's the easiest way I can paint the picture for you. Madison relies on tech. Let's not give her what she relies on." Reggie responds.

"Okay, Noted," Yohan adds.

I am filled with so many questions, but I choose to ask the most important one because if we are going to be working with them and have Madison out of the picture, I need to know how we will keep her oblivious.

"But how will we communicate if she's all in our texts and calls, popping up on our screens?"

I see a smile widening on Quinn's face.

"We take it old school, baby! I think this is a good meeting spot, but we don't want to make it a habit. She might be annoying, but she's smart. I say we leave notes under that gargoyle in the front of the bakery so we can swap ideas and finalize our plan. Collect as much information as you can. We have to move fast."

"As far as getting her there, don't worry. Once we come up with a plan and set a date, we'll tell her we've been taking the initiative and making our own threats and that we've gotten you guys to meet up with all of us."

"But won't she want proof? Of us, like agreeing?"

Reggie chimes in, "Trust me, Madison's logic doesn't work like that. Once she hears she's getting what she wants, that's her only concern; the details that get her there are minuscule."

Lexie looks at me, then Yohan and I see we are all on the same page.

Patra returns with our shots, and we raise our glasses in cheers for our newly devised plan.

I take my Scythe Wielder shot like a pro with the others, and I am actually surprised I've been able to keep all this alcohol down without vomiting or making a complete fool of myself for once.

I guess I'm really evolving.

With my newly found confidence fueled by vampire-themed cocktails and cookie-inspired sugary whiskey, I stand up and decide to make a statement to make this official.

"All right, guys, let's do this: operation take down Madison in full effect."

I reach my arm in the middle of the table and wait for the others to join.

The fists all come connecting at the center of the table, and I know this is it.

Madison is going down.

Chapter Thirteen

Yohan

Knock Knock

My head is pounding.

This is why they say don't mix liquors.

Knock Knock

"Come in, Pa," I yell and sit up on the side of my bed.

My dad walks in with a massive smile on his face, and I'm happy because, for once, I know he's not here to give me a speech about how I need to get my life together.

We have a pretty good relationship, and it's not that he's always on my case, but when he mentions the things I should have done in my past to have a better situation now, I tend to feel guilty because a part of me knows he's right.

"Hey, Yo, long night last night, huh? You came in pretty late."

"Yeah, I just went out with a few friends from work to catch up, that's all."

He takes a seat next to me and places his hand on my shoulder.

"It's good to see you making friends so quickly here. You know it was hard with the past moves, watching you stay in your room all the time constantly on the computer or drawing and blasting that heavy metal music."

"Yeah, well, I might have made friends pretty quickly here, but don't expect the music to go away. I'm metal till I die, Pa, metal till I die."

"Ha-ha, I know. I would be wondering who the hell is this imposter in my son's room if I didn't hear the occasional angry band leader screaming out the stereo."

He lets out a small laugh before I see his face take on a sterner expression.

"But I do need to talk to you about something, Yohan."

"What's up, Pa?"

"Well, you know that job I've been trying to get into for the past three years, constantly sending in applications, updating my resume, and being shut down?"

"The one over in Lilac Bay?"

His smile grows wide across his face.

"That's the one. I don't know what changed, maybe because I never gave up. Maybe because I've gotten more experience under my belt, maybe a great reference? I don't know, and I'm really not going to question it. All I know is I'm happy because finally, Yohan, I finally got it."

I can't help but instantly reach over to hug my father. I am so genuinely happy for him. If anyone deserves a lucky break, it's him. He's done so much for me and our family, and I'm so happy the universe is paying it forward.

"Oh my God! Pa! I'm so happy for you. You've wanted this job for as long as I can remember, and the salary, the salary, must be so much more than you're making now. You'll be able to do more of the things you want."

"We will, Yohan, both of us. We're going to have a substantially better life, but we're going to have to move, just one last time."

I try not to react in any way that might kill his joy, so I keep my facial expression from showing what I truly feel inside and force a smile.

"Hey, we've done it before. We'll do it again. One last time."

"I knew you'd be happy, and honestly, Yohan, I really am sorry to keep doing this to you. I know you like it here, and I see you making friends, and you even found a job you like, but after this, there will be so many more opportunities for you in Lilac Bay."

"Maybe you can invite your friends over for a celebration, and it's not a goodbye. They can always come to visit us out there. Trust me, it'll be a hell of an upgrade from this dump."

Yeah, because they can just get up and travel miles away.

"Sure thing, Pa, I'll ask."

He gets up and makes his way to the door, "We did it, Yohan, we finally made it." He raises his fist in a congratulatory manner, closes the door, and exits my room.

Well, that's one way to start the day.

I really am genuinely happy for my father, but I really like it here. I like the friends I've made, the magic that lives here, the guy I met.

I can't leave.

I can't abandon Lexie and Ella. They are counting on me just as much as I am counting on them, and we are stronger as a group. If we separate, who knows what Madison will do? One thing is for sure: things need to speed up.

We need a solution, and we need it now.

I grab my phone and shoot a text over to Max. With all the things going on, I completely forgot to reach out to him as a resource, and with the clocking ticking by and picking up speed, I need all the help I can get.

> Hey Max, it's been a long time. Need to talk. Maybe call me when you get a chance? It's important.

I throw my phone on my bed and gather my things for work. I'm leaving early so I can walk today, swing by the bakery, and check the gargoyle.

I know it's only been a few hours, but who knows? Maybe Quinn and Reggie pulled an all-nighter, and there is an intricate scheme all written out and just waiting for us to fine-tune and reply to.

I take a quick shower, get dressed, grab my things, and make my way down the stairs of my building.

As I approach the door, I see none other than Nash waiting outside, leaning up against the building, casually vaping.

Is he waiting for me?

Probably Not.

I gather my nerves and tell my anxiety to take a back seat.

If I like this guy, I need to at least talk to him.

Hell, if I want to be friends with this guy, I need to at least talk to him.

I would've texted him, but the design isn't finished yet. I haven't even had time to start it. Ever since this whole Aidens spiral adventure started, my art has suffered severely all around. I haven't drawn anything in days.

What would I even text him about, anyway?

With my nerves as settled as they are ever going to be, I push the door open and decide for once I will make the first attempt to approach him.

I mean, he can't think it's weird to say hi, right?

I think it would be weirder to just walk right past him.

"Hey, Nash," I say, trying to sound as casual as possible and hoping I'm not flushing or seeming awkward.

"Yohan, just the guy I was hoping to see. How are you? Heading to work?"

"Yeah, heading out early today, you know. Just decided to walk and clear my head a bit."

He doesn't care. Why are you telling him that?

"Totally. Fall's my favorite time of year, you know, spooky season, the color of the leaves. I'm sure, as an artist, you totally can appreciate that."

His voice is so mellow, and everything he does is just smooth. He makes everything look just so easy.

I wish my personality was like that.

"Yeah, it's my favorite time of year too, you know, got a love for Halloween and stuff," I respond.

"Yeah, it's freaking awesome. Are you getting into character this year? I'm sure you would come up with something sick." He says as he continues to puff his vape.

"No, kind of pressed for time this year, plus I probably won't be around that long. Most likely will end up moving again."

He furrows his brow.

He does care.

"Oh Man, that sucks. We were just getting to know each other, but I get it. I think you mentioned before your dad's job, right?"

"Yeah, story of my life." I sigh.

"It's okay, man. Well, hopefully, you'll like the next place you move to. Do you think I'll at least get that design before you go?"

"Of course, I keep my promises."

Oh God, that sounded flirtatious.

"Ha-ha, good to know. Well, I don't want to make you late for work or anything."

"Yeah, I should probably get going."

"Got it, but before you go, I wanted to show you something. I totally jumped the gun here on this, getting my first tattoo and all, but I wanted to get something to see what the pain level was like before I had you finish that piece for me."

"No way, you got your first piece?"

I love art, but I love tattoos even more. They tell a lot about a person, and I can't wait to see what little detail I find out about Nash from whatever he's chosen.

He lifts his shirt a bit to reveal a tattoo on his rib cage, and I cannot believe what I am seeing.

It can't be.

A black rose.

It's a coincidence. It has to be a coincidence.

I'm frozen.

"What, you don't like it?" he says, looking worried.

"No, I love it... I mean, it's cool, totally cool." I say, trying to recover.

"Yeah, and it didn't even really hurt. I sat like a champ." He lowers his shirt back down.

"Cool, so catch up later. I really have to head to work."

"Yeah, totally. See you on the weekend, Yo-Yo."

I head down the street, mind spinning and trying to maintain my composure.

Oh my God, what is happening in my life?

Is this real?

Does it mean anything?

Is this guy my soul mate?

Something that doesn't exist, the black rose.

What?

I try to focus on my next task at hand and put Nash at the back of my mind for now. I'll bring it up to the girls later and see what they think, but for now, I need to get to the bakery and check the gargoyle.

If I even have a chance of having a love life, or any regular life for that matter, I'm going to need to get this girl Madison off my case.

I make it to the bakery rather quickly and try not to look suspicious as I approach the gargoyle stationed at the front of the building. Still, of course, I'm naturally awkward, so anything I do looks suspicious, anyway.

At first, I spot nothing, but as I move toward the back, I see a pink envelope stamped with a heart peeking just slightly out the back of one of the gargoyle's wings.

I grab the envelope quickly and keep it moving, heading towards work.

When I finally arrive at FURNISH, I make my way to my usual department, or at least I try to, before Jaden abruptly stops me.

"Hey, Yohan, So I know you haven't been scheduled for a meeting yet, but we are starting rotation today. You will be training in Kitchens."

Seriously, my brain is overloaded with a million things, and now this?

I barely know Home Offices.

"Okay, no problem."

I head over to Kitchens, where I see Rose waiting for me, and I have to say I am less than pleased to have to spend the day with her because her tone always seems dry, and her personality is non-existent.

On top of it, I can tell she is one of those people who is constantly judging me in her head.

But hey, I need a job, so I'll deal.

"Hello, Yohan, separated from your little friends today, huh? Don't worry, I'll make it fun."

"Can't wait," I respond, forcing a smile.

I spend most of the day shadowing her with customers and taking mental notes of what they might need, what services we have, and how to quickly find smaller catalog items such as silverware, pots, pans, and other knick-knacks the masochists, as Lexie likes to call them might be looking for.

As she's going over the options we have for cabinet combinations, my phone pings, and I'm hoping it's from Lexie and Aella. I didn't realize until today how fortunate I am to work with them because, without their company, this day is dragging.

I pull my phone from my pocket and swipe up to reveal a text from the Haus of Ascension grouper.

Smoker's spot on break? I hate it here in Bedrooms. I'm getting hit on here more than ever. You are so lucky you get to stay in Home Offices Lex.

Girl, we're witches now. Just use your powers and fling those thirst buckets into the
wall with your psychic abilities. Ha-ha, J.K., I
miss you guys! Totally in for a meeting at the
smoker's spot.

I'll be there. Rose is driving me freaking nuts.
How can you be so… boring?

Aelia

That's easy, just be Rose.

Lexie

Lol. Facts.

I look up from my phone and notice Rose uncomfortably close and staring into my soul.

"Yohan, one of the most significant rules we have here is no phones on the sales floor. You know that. You've been through basic train-ing. The customer comes first. They must have your full attention always."

"Sorry, Rose," I say, showing my teeth in what I'm trying to sell as a smile.

It's quickly followed by the most giant eye roll I can muster up as soon as she turns her back and continues her long speech about all the wonderful possibilities of cabinet combinations FURNISH has to offer.

The hours drag on, but thankfully, the time for break finally ar-rives.

I try to remember the path to the smoker's spot that Lexie and Ella took me on that day, but it's not long before I spot them walking together ahead of me.

"You guys back here," I call out, and I see them turn and make their way towards me.

"Mr. Yohan, hey," Lexie says as she approaches me and begins to walk at my side.

"So, how was Kitchens with Rose?" "Tell us all about it," Ella adds, now joining my vacant side.

"Yeah, eff Rose, and screw Kitchens, we've got so much more to talk about."

They looked shocked, and I continue.

I've been holding this all in for hours, and I feel like I'm about to burst.

"First off, I stopped by the bakery and got this."

I pull the pink envelope from my pocket and hold it in the air.

"Yohan, before you go any further." Lexie holds her phone down by her side and directs her eyes to it, which reminds me we need to be careful when discussing anything pertaining to Madison.

She could be eavesdropping through any device.

"Yeah, you're right, Lex. Let's take a moment to decompress from this hell of a day, and then we'll talk." Ella says, widening her eyes dramatically, as if Madison could see us.

We continue our walk silently while powering off our phones and when we finally get to our official lunch spot. The conversation commences immediately.

"Omg, open it Yohan." Lexie says, basically hovering over the table where the pink letter now sits.

"Yeah, what are you waiting for? I'm sorry, but if it was me who had stopped there, I would've totally read it and filled you guys in."

"Yeah, same," Lexie adds.

"Okay, here goes nothing," I rip open the envelope, revealing a small letter in barely legible handwriting. If I had to make an educated guess,

I would say Quinn picked the envelope, and Reggie wrote the note, but who knows, it could totally be vice versa.

"Well, read it already." Ella blurts out, clearly showcasing impatience as one of her personality traits that I failed to pick up on.

"It says Ellington Park, two days, 10 pm. Practice what you have. We will, too."

"The hell? That's it?" Lexie says, now snatching the paper away.

"That's pretty vague. So much for them being a reliable resource."

"Well, I mean, they're our only resource, so we have to kind of go with the flow but be on our toes, you know? It doesn't take a rocket scientist to know that you probably shouldn't put all your trust in someone you met one night in a bar." I profess, hoping to get my point across.

"True, but has Madison attempted to contact either of you today? I find it so weird that after we meet Reggie and Quinn, she's extremely silent. Shouldn't she be threatening us by now?".

"Well, she hasn't attempted to contact me at all, just you guys so far, and to be honest, we have been kind of shutting our phones off from time to time. Maybe she's just tired of being ignored. She seems like that would get to her."

"You've got a point, Ella. I hope you're right, and I hope it's not because she's planning something on a bigger scale, because I've been practicing the spiral and all, but still nothing."

"Also, I've got some not-so-great news... I'm leaving." I say, afraid of what their responses will be.

They're going to think I'm running because I'm afraid. I'm not afraid.

I want to stay.

"No, the hell you're not. You can't just leave us here in this mess. This crap only started when you got here, so if you're leaving, you're leaving when it's fixed!" Lexie says, obviously fuming at the idea of me leaving them in the middle of all this alone.

"It's not that I want to leave. It's my dad. He got another new job, the one he wanted for years, a permanent one. He actually feels a little bad that we are leaving again. I think he wants to meet you guys. He asked me to invite you guys over."

"Whelp, looks like we're just going to have to figure this out sooner than later," Ella adds, completely dismissing my invitation.

I can tell she's trying to keep her cool, but I don't think the idea of me leaving without helping them find a solution to any of this is sitting well with her, either.

"Listen, I won't leave until this is fixed, I promise. I'm sure I can figure something out, but I'm here now, and we need to get going. What should we say back to Reggie and Quinn?"

I'm pretty sure Lexie was waiting for me to ask this question because her response is swift and pointed.

"I say if they're going to play all secretive and give us a short little note, we do the same. We simply say okay, practice what we've got, and show up guns blazing."

"Practice what we have? Do you mean like another wishing spell?" Ella asks, eyes hopeful.

"Yeah, no, none of that, at least not at my house. I caught Xyla trying to reenact our séance the other day. I was less than pleased. Also, I think we should figure out the ins and outs before we just go calling things to ourselves. That's how we got stuck with Madison in the first place."

"Good point," I add.

It gets a little quiet, and I can tell we're all in our own thoughts. We've all had a rough couple of days, and it would be just cool to unwind to take a break.

I think about lightening the mood a bit, even though I hate being vulnerable, but if I have to go back and spend my day in Kitchens with Rose, I could use a laugh with friends, and this conversation has been a little tense.

Okay, Yohan, you can do this.

"So, I know you guys are a little annoyed with me right now, but I have an update on Nash or whatever."

They both turn to me and smile, and I can tell it's not me they're mad at.

They just don't want me to leave, at least not yet.

It kind of feels good. These are really my friends.

"Squee! Omg, tell us," Ella says, now bouncing in her seat.

"Yes, you should've led with that Yo-Yo. Remember piping hot tea first. The rest can wait."

I'm smiling, I'm nervous, I'm blushing, I can just tell.

"Okay, so on my way here, I ran into him, and we were talking, you know, basic stuff, mostly about the design and whatnot…"

"Omg, did he kiss you?" Ella blurts out, which triggers Lexie's giggling.

"No, no, but he had a tattoo, his first one, and he showed it to me. You wouldn't believe what it was.."

"If you say a black rose, I'm going to die…" Ella says, now leaning closer.

"It was, it was a black rose."

"Lexie, that's it. Call the morgue. I'm dead. This magic stuff is just laying it on thick, huh?"

"Girl, well, where's my love story? Shit, I was there too, Hello Universe! Over here, hook a girl up!" Lexie says, now waving her hand in the air.

I can't help but chuckle.

Lexie scoots over and reaches in, now hugging me. "No, but seriously, Yohan, I am so happy for you. See now, you really can't leave, at least not now. Things are just getting good."

"Also, side note, when do we get to meet Nash? Maybe he's our fourth."

"And I'm the one who watches too many movies?" Ella quickly comments.

"But I do have an idea not to ignore your dad's invite over or anything. We can totally do that, too, but I think we should have a movie night, maybe a sleepover since I have this apartment to myself. It gets super boring, not like my brothers were there much, to begin with, but it's kind of a drag having the place so empty all the time."

"Oh my gosh, yes, girl, I could use a distraction from all this b. s, and speaking of drag, we could totally check out your brothers on that show. It would be fun."

"Yeah, sure," Ella responds as unenthusiastically as possible.

"Maybe you can invite Nash over too, you know, just for a bit, so we can meet him if that's cool with you, Ella."

"Of course, Duh, I want to meet him too."

"I'm in, and I'll shoot Nash a text."

A night out doesn't sound bad, plus if I do end up leaving, I want to spend as much time with them as possible. You don't meet people you naturally click with this quickly often in life, and this, this is my tribe.

"Yay! Adult sleepover at my place. Tomorrow night good?"

"Can we not call it that? It sounds creepy." Lexie adds, now raising an eyebrow.

"Yeah, kind of has weird vibes,"

"Okay, okay, an adult slumber party?"

"Let's just say we're hanging out," I say, trying to save Ella quickly from Lexie's next comment.

"Now that sounds normal."

A night at Ella's will definitely help us all get away from the drama for a bit.

It's the perfect opportunity for us to put together a plan and not feel so alone.

This gives us time to work together, have some fun, and tackle this mess.

After all, time is running out.

Two days and it's go-time.

Two days, and Madison's going down.

Chapter Fourteen

Lexie

God, today was such a long day at work.

The green binders are back, and now the masochists are asking for more color options for tabletops...

When does it end?

Okay, focus, Lex.

Just a couple more things.

"Ms. Cookie Dough check, phone check, house key check."

Okay, I think that's everything.

I make my way to my mirror and check my outfit. I know we're staying in, but that doesn't mean I don't want to look good.

Besides, I need to stop at Eat Your Heart Bakery to drop off our note, and you never know, I might meet Mr. Right in the process.

Hey, magic worked for Yohan. It might be trying to assist me behind the scenes, too, and I'm more than willing to do my part.

Looking good, Lex. Better get um girl. Hmm... but maybe I should change this top.

"Hey, Lexie, are we going to watch that movie tonight? I've been waiting for you, but everyone in my class has already seen it, and it's getting harder and harder to avoid spoilers."

"Omg, Xyla, you scared me."

Do people knock anymore?

I really need to start locking my door.

"Sorry, Lex, I just saw the door cracked, and I saw you standing there, so I didn't think you'd mind."

I notice the dispirited look on her face, and I immediately try to soften my tone.

"No, no, it's ok, but I'll have to put that movie night on hold Xy."

"I'm sorry I've just been having a lot of stuff going on, but I promise, as soon as everything is back to normal, not only will we have a movie night, we'll have a mystery movie marathon."

"Ok," she replies, head hanging in disappointment and exiting my room.

The guilt from not spending time with my sister has been in the back of my mind constantly lately. I remember how it was to be young and wanting to have someone to look up to, someone to spend time with, but if I don't get all this magic stuff figured out, things might get worse.

Madison might even end up targeting her, and that is one thing I will not allow to happen.

Once I'm finally pleased with my outfit and have everything packed, I decide to walk over to the bakery. If anything, I can catch a Dryve from there, which will be cheaper, but also, I want to enjoy the scenery.

It's coming close to Halloween, so most of the houses in town are all decked out in elaborate decorations, some animated, some creepily realistic, and some just playful and fun.

I've always loved this time of year for its effortless, magical essence, but I never in a million years thought I would end up being magical, which lately I've been questioning altogether.

I feel like I have little to offer in this whole situation.

There's Yo-Yo with his spiral, which was clearly meant for him, seeing as how he had information on the whole thing before he even met us, and Aella now with her visions. But me, I have nothing.

I'm still the same Lexie.

With all these thoughts whirling around in my head, I try to piece together what my actual role in all of this is as I continue my walk.

It's not long before I approach Eat Your Heart Out bakery and pull our envelope with our response to Quinn and Reggie out of my pocket, the simple note displaying one word: OK.

It's not as fancy as the one Quinn and Reggie left. Ours is plain and white, similar to what you would use to hold a greeting card or an old-fashioned handwritten letter, but to add a bit of flare, I added a little heart to emulate the one left on the original envelope as a sign of unity.

A reminder that we are in this together with a common goal: to take down Madison.

I try to remember where Yohan said he found their first letter, and I'm pretty sure he said he found it behind one of the wings, so I stick the letter behind the large gargoyle's stone wing with just the hint of white from the envelope visible.

Once the letter is placed, I take a seat near the front entrance while I request a Dryve and go digging for my hairbrush for a shot of whiskey while I wait.

The place is pretty dead tonight, from what I can tell.

It's not like it's always overly packed, but I just have a weird feeling. I don't know why, but I can't shake it, and the longer I sit here, the worse it gets.

Just as I find my hairbrush, unscrew the bottom, and am about to take my shot, I hear a voice come from behind me.

"Don't you guys usually travel in threes? Well, lately, anyway."

Why is everyone always sneaking up on me?

I turn around and realize it's Patra, the creepy waitress, puffing on a cigarette and being just all around weird as usual.

"Oh hey, yeah, I was just going for a walk, actually heading to meet my friends now."

"Ah, I see. My bar's not good enough for you guys anymore?"

Wait what?

"No, no, not that at all. Wait, your bar? You own the place?"

Then why is she always waiting tables?

"I do, and before you ask, I like to be on the floor to get to know my customers. You know I pride myself on creating friendly spaces for all. I see everything, and when things go left, people, they are uninvited."

What is she insinuating? I don't even want to know. This lady is creepy.

"Good to know," I respond, trying to sound as genuine as possible.

"Do you guys like it here? My bar? Are there any suggestions you might have to make it more appealing?" she asks as she continues to puff smoke like a human chimney.

"No, not at all. I mean, the food is good, the drinks are so unique, and… Oh, look, sorry, my ride."

I have never been so happy to see my Dryve appear.

"Okay, see you soon, Lexie… hopefully."

Get away from her. She's nuts.

I make my way to my Dryve, greet the driver, and let out a sigh of relief to ease the tension of that awkward conversation.

The Dryve ride is quiet, my favorite kind.

I just get so annoyed with the drivers who talk incessantly about the things going on in their lives as if you know them personally and you don't have your own things going on.

When I finally pull up to Ella's place, I notice her and Yohan outside talking on the front porch of her apartment, probably waiting for me, and I couldn't make it out of the car any faster.

"The party's here!" I announce as I adjust my outfit and do a spin for added dramatics.

I have to make an entrance. Ella's not the only one who can walk down an aisle like it's a runway in fashion week. I decide to give her a run for her money as I strut, turn, and serve my way to the front door.

We make our way inside, and I tell them about my weird little conversation with Patra as Ella makes us all drinks, and we make our way to her sofa.

"Yeah, apparently, she owns the place, but that's beside the point. She was being all weird saying she sees everything and people can be uninvited, blah blah blah."

"Well, since she sees EVERYTHING, hopefully, she sees how weird she is." Yohan comments, which causes Ella to spit out a bit of her drink and giggle.

"Hopefully, but down to business. Have either of you heard from our blonde-haired arch-nemesis?"

"Nope."

"Not at all, and I haven't even been powering my phone off. I say we just enjoy the night and forget about her, for now, at least. We already have a time slot set up to deal with her."

Just as Yohan finishes his statement, his phone pings.

Here we go, we went and talked her up. Either that, or she's eavesdropping. I Wouldn't be surprised.

"Okay, what did she say?"

"Uh, it's not her."

"Ooouuu, is that Nash? Did you text him? Will he be joining us?"

"No, not him either. It's weird. I went to text him, but I couldn't find his number. I didn't overthink it because we live in the same building. I figured Madison deleted it from my phone or something."

"But anyway, it's from neither of them. It's from Max." He wrinkles his brow.

Even better, it's an actual resource that knows at least a little something about all this magic stuff.

"What did he say?"

"Yeah, does he have any advice?"

"He said verbatim, *Yohan, please leave me the hell alone. I want nothing to do with this. Do not text me. Do not reach out to me. This is YOUR problem.* Emphasis on the your part."

"It's so weird, though, because his personality is not even like that at all. Aside from that, I didn't even tell him what I needed."

"This has Madison written all over it."

"Yeah, she must have gotten to him first,"

Ella stands up from the couch and makes her way to the center of the room, clearly frustrated.

"Okay, you guys! This is our night to have fun and let loose before we face the beast head-on. I say let's have some fun. Should we lighten the mood a bit and check out this drag show my brothers are on, or what? If drag queens can't help us let loose, I don't know what can."

It's funny how she's suddenly all wanting to watch Bixie's. The other night, she seemed like that was the last thing she wanted to do.

Maybe she's just lonely in the house like she said, and she's happy to have people over.

Or maybe she misses her brothers, and it's a chance to see them and be happy for them.

Maybe it's both.

My thought process is interrupted when she finally gets the show going, and it's already started. Seems to be about a quarter way through. One of the live battles is currently happening with two queens going head-to-head lip-syncing to some pop song from the early 2000s.

It is exceptionally entertaining to see the queens spin, twirl, and death drop, all while completely changing their outfits, including wigs.

I look over to Yohan to see if he's enjoying the show, and he seems just as into it as Ella and I, laughing and eyes widening at the drag queen's antics.

I just can't help but think that no matter what all this means, in the end, I know I was supposed to meet them, that somehow our lives are tied together, that this is all fated, and it adds to my confidence, I am no longer questioning how we will get through this magical mess.

I just know we will.

Bixie announces the winner of the previous head-to-head competition and dismisses the losing queen to the back of the stage. She then announces the next pair set up to battle.

"All right, what an amazing performance from Ms. Itza Matza-Kure. I think we need to start taking her name literally because, honey, slay, she did!"

The audience roars in agreement.

"Up next, we have two newer queens who have been dying to make a name for themselves since they arrived. Please welcome to the stage Penny ILuv Vodka and Imma Manduh."

"Omg, look, Ella, it's Aeden and Aesher!"

I must admit I am kind of fangirling a bit, seeing her brothers on TV.

Not only that, God, their bodies look good, literally glistening, as they walk down the stage holding up the signs with each of the opposing queen's names displayed, leading the performers to the center platform.

I totally should have gone on that date with Aeden when he told me he liked me. Or wait, was that Aesher?

Oh crap.

"Can they at least put some more clothes on? Geez, it's gross."

"Yohan over there doesn't seem to mind." I throw him a wink, and he turns red.

I turn my attention back to the TV where both the queens are now standing center stage, silk hoods covering their faces; I guess it adds to the drama of the show, you know, the big reveal.

The crowd gets quiet. "Okay, let's put that beauty on display. It's time to slay my queens, flip those hoods, and reveal yourselves!".

Both queens simultaneously draw back their hoods, and their makeup is stunning, flawless actually, and I...

"OH MY GOSH, Bash, it's Bash! Penny is Bash!" Yohan says, jumping out of his seat.

"Bash your friend that went missing?"

"Yes, oh my God, that's him. The message he left, he said they were using magic, he needed help, he was in trouble."

"Yohan, calm down!"

"No, Lexie, this is not a time to be calm. Do you hear what he's saying?"

"That means that it's not only Bash that's in trouble, but my brothers as well. I wondered why they hadn't called or checked in or anything. I know we didn't leave on the best terms, but it's not like them...I felt it. We're triplets, remember? It must be why my mood has been so off."

No. No. No.

Not more things to deal with.

We already have a crazy tech witch on our case whose friends are trying to betray her, who we are for some reason, putting all our trust in...

And now...

Now, drag queens who are kidnapping people and are also witches? Where's the button?

Where's Rewind? Because I can't.

I cannot.

"I have to help Bash. We have to go there! He's always helped me. I can't leave him alone like that. He sounded so scared, and we'll help get your brothers out too; as far as I'm concerned, we're all family now; we have to do this."

I have never seen Yohan be so serious. He usually has such a carefree or nervous type of energy, but this is different. He means business. He really cares about this guy and is willing to take risks.

"Well, I guess we're headed to wherever the hell they are," I say, trying to sound confident.

"It's a live show, so I'm sure we can find the address. People buy tickets all the time. It'll be getting past security and backstage. That will be the issue."

"Screw it. We'll even try the wishing spell again if we have to, but we'll have to handle Madison first. That goes down tomorrow. Bash and your brothers should be safe until then. It's a live show. They can't actually disappear until the end of the season; it would cause too much suspicion, so we have a little time."

"Okay, agreed. Madison first, drag queens next."

"What have we gotten ourselves into, you guys?"

"I don't know, but we're in deep now. Yo-Yo, do you think we can watch that video Bash sent you? Maybe it will help us piece some things together."

"Yeah, sure, I have it saved on my laptop. I've been watching it, trying to zoom in on little fragments to find clues myself. Maybe you guys can swing by tomorrow before we meet Madison, and we can all sift through it. Three brains are better than one."

"Also, I know we're dealing with a lot, but my dad really wants to meet you guys, so if you guys are cool with it, maybe I can introduce you. He just likes to know my friends, plus with us leaving soon, time is limited. He did already mention that you guys are invited to visit anytime, though he says he can already tell I've met some good friends this time around."

"Aww, your dad sounds so sweet, Yohan. I like him already."

"Aww, he does. I don't know If I'll be able to make it, though. I have work in the am."

"Girl, just call out. Did you really plan on going into that damn furniture store when we have an entire plan to devise?"

"True, yeah, I'll be there. Jaden can figure it out."

"Yeah, Mr., all my brown nosing finally paid off, and now I'm manager ass Jaden," I say mockingly.

We all laugh. It's clear we share the same annoyance for Jaden, not that he is not a nice guy, but geez, do you do anything besides think of FURNISH all day? If so, what is it? Because I can't tell.

"Okay, you guys, as host of this sleepover, I mean uh hang out at night thing, I say magic and work talk aside, let's get back to the fun and less planning. What movie are we thinking?"

"Something witchy!" I suggest teasingly.

"Yeah, let's not."

"How about a Rom-Com?" Yohan suggests bashfully.

"Okay, Mr. Yohan, Nash got you all in your feels over there, huh?"

"Maybe."

"Ha-ha, you're so cute, Yo-Yo." I toss a pillow at him.

"Oh My Gosh, they have Little Tragedies. I love this one! You guys in?"

"Yes! I just love Shayla. She's so me."

"I've never seen it."

Me and Ella look at each other, quickly stand, get into character, and the quote spills out immediately:

"How do I feel?"

"HOW DO I FEEL?"

"I feel like a gourmet buffet, honey, because all you bitches can eat me!"

Yohan's eyes expand before he bursts into laughter, nearly spilling his drink.

"Okay, sounds funny, I'm in."

The rest of the night goes by effortlessly while we watch movies, eat snacks, make drinks, and discuss anything and everything aside from magic and mysticism.

As we're winding down and getting ready to call it a night, we hear our phones ping simultaneously, which causes our now dwindling conversation to pick up pace.

It's the grouper; if we're all here, that means only one thing.

Madison.

I reach for my phone and open the text thread.

Haus of Ascension

Madison

> Really? I still haven't been included in the Haus of Ascension grouper? How utterly rude.

Madison

> Just a little reminder: tomorrow at ten, be there.

Madison

> Or save me the trouble, video call me, and will me the pages.

Madison

> Oh, no? We already tried that, huh?

Madison

> Okay, well, see you tomorrow, love ya.

"Should we even bother responding?"

"No, let's not let her ruin our night. I'm getting tired. You guys, let's end on a good note."

"Yeah, you're right. Screw her."

"Yeah, screw her," Yohan agrees with a yawn.

"You know, this isn't that bad. Think about it." I can't help but mimic Yohan's yawn, now feeling even more exhausted.

"We're kind of lucky, you know, to be witches and all," I say, eyes closing while I shift my body on the couch and adjust my blanket.

"Yeah, we are."

"Hashtag Blessed." Ella yawns.

"Depends on which way you look at it, either hashtag blessed or hashtag cursed."

He makes a good point...

I can barely keep my eyes open.

As I begin to give in to my body and let sleep have its way, I can't help but think.

It ends tomorrow.

I know one thing: there's absolutely no way I'm claiming cursed as a hashtag.

That is just not going to happen.

Not now, not ever.

#Period.

CHAPTER FIFTEEN

Yohan

I CAN'T BELIEVE IT'S here.

Today is the day she goes down.

We're coming for you, Madison.

My mind is overrun with so many possibilities of how today could turn out. We don't really have much to work with and are relying heavily on Quinn and Reggie.

I hope we can really trust them.

The most I can do is try to practice the spiral, which I have been doing, but I have had little success.

A considerable part of me feels like the weight of this problem with Madison rests heavily on my shoulders, seeing as how the spiral has somehow become my responsibility and seems like the only thing we really have that we can use besides the protection we already wished for.

I have to admit it makes me feel a sense of guilt because I have been unsuccessful so far, and with the clock ticking and our meeting only hours away, I feel hope is lost; I feel useless.

Am I just leading everyone to our defeat?

What is she really capable of?

She wouldn't really kill us, would she?

A part of me has seriously been considering trying to talk Lexie into just willing her the pages.

Willing her the pages would allow us all just to forget this ever happened. We could walk back into our regular lives and leave this magic stuff behind.

In all honesty, the purpose of all of this doesn't even make complete sense to me. From what I've gathered, it's some type of game for power, power in the afterlife, which none of us knows anything about.

So why does everyone want it?

Whatever the case may be, I know I still need to practice.

I reach for my phone, open the screenshot Lexie sent to me, and give it another scan. I have to be missing something.

Aidens Spiral

Used for protection, symbolizes protection by fire.

Can protect an individual from advanced forms of magic.

Use with caution.

Due to Aiden's Spiral's association with fire, its projection is known to cause adverse heat-related effects, permanent delusion, and, in extreme cases, DEATH.

****

Use is only intended for the pure of heart.

Only those whose intentions come from a childlike place of innocence may obtain and use this ability.

Summoning Aiden's Spiral

Aiden's spiral requires advanced visualization.

See the jagged spiral in the mind's eye, focus on the center,

will it to spin, as it spins, envision the spiral beginning to

light at its end, and project your intent into the spiral.

Make the spiral yours.

Charge it with your essence, with your will.

Release the Spiral and your intent at your target once the

flame reaches the end.

Trust in the universe and release all fear.

Ugh, this is so frustrating!

No matter how many times I try to read it, it all looks the same; everything just blurs together, and I can't figure out what I could be missing.

What don't I see?

What am I doing wrong?

I try to shake away the thoughts of failure, close my eyes, stand, and have another try.

Focus on the center of the Spiral.

Spin, Spiral, Spin.

My intent is protection.

My intent is to keep her from hurting us.

Ignite for me, spiral!

I see the spark of a flame at the end of the spiral, and this is new.

It's farther than I've gotten before, but just as the flame ignites at the spiral's end, I feel my body begin to get hot.

Ignore it, Yohan.

They need you.

My intent is protection.

MY INTENT IS TO KEEP HER FROM HURTING US!

The flame continues to dance at the end of the spiral but is not moving through the spiral, and it is not spinning as I expected it to.

It's not like I envisioned, and I continue to get hot.

I can feel the sweat dripping down my face, my breath getting heavy, and I'm starting to get dizzy, but I refuse to stop.

I can't, I won't. This is all my fault.

I SAID SPIN!

ping

I snap out of my daze at the sound of the alert from my phone and drop to my knees instantly, so weak, out of breath, and hot.

I take a second to bring myself back to the world. The space in my mind where I was seemed so far, dark, and honestly scary.

I don't know what I've gotten myself into. What are we going to do? If I can't even get this damn spiral to spin, how are we ever going to stop Madison or save Bash?

I need this to work; it just has to.

ping

I reach for my phone, finally feeling back to normal, and swipe at my notifications.

It's the Haus of Ascension grouper.

Hey, Yo-Yo, what time were you thinking?

Are you that dense girl? Just scroll up. I said it was 10 pm tonight.

Lexie

Don't you have anything better to do, Madison?

Madison

Well, if you would just will me the pages, you guys can play Haus of Ascension games all day, and I'll be out of your hair.

Aella

We're not giving you a damn thing. We've told you several times, Madison, it looks like you're the one who's dense.

Madison

Oh, look, Ms. Aella grew a pair overnight and now has some sass behind a phone screen.

Madison

Keep that same energy, bitch! I dare you.

Lexie

I am going to kick your ass when I see you in person, so YOU keep that same energy, Madison. You do not know who you're playing with.

I am ignoring the troll. Anytime is fine. Call when here.

I slide my phone into my pocket and ignore the pings. I don't want to be involved in their catfight because who knows how long that will last, and I can use this time to get the place cleaned up before they arrive.

I spend about an hour or two tidying up my room, mostly because I figured that's where we could hang out and review the video Bash sent me while we devise our game plan for tonight.

As I'm in the kitchen looking for snacks to put out for us, my phone rings, and I can't help but get excited that they are here.

Our friendship is the only thing that I think is keeping me sane right now. Everything else just seems so draining.

I answer the call, quickly throw on my shoes, and make my way down to the front entrance to let them in so we can start planning this day that I know is going to take a toll on us all, essentially.

"Hey there, Yohan,"

"Hey Lex, Hey Ella,"

"Haus of Ascension, it's the big day!"

"Yes, Operation take down Madison in full effect."

"Shh," I exclaim, waving my phone as a reminder.

Lexie rolls her eyes. "I cannot wait until this crap is over."

We make our way upstairs and into my apartment, where I notice my dad rushing around and swearing to himself while grabbing his things and stuffing them into his pockets.

"Uh, hey, Dad, this is Lexie and Aella, my friends from work I was telling you about."

"Oh hey, it's so nice to meet you. Yohan has told me so much about you."

"Good things, I hope," Lexie states while tilting her head.

"Only good things, of course. I told him when we leave, I would love for you guys to visit. Yohan says he's loved it here so far, and I'm sure you girls are a big part of the reason why."

"Aww, Yo-Yo, you've made it awesome for us, too," Ella says, smirking.

My dad throws his jacket on and looks at me with a guilty grin. "So, Yohan, I am so happy I have gotten to meet your friends, but I got called into work at the last minute, so it will just be you guys."

He turns to Lexie and Ella. "Sorry to make this such a short first meeting, but enjoy yourselves. Please help yourself with anything you need. I'm sure Yohan will be a great host."

"No problem. Nice meeting you, Mr. Vazquez."

"Yes, nice meeting you."

"Nice meeting you girls, too. See you later, Yohan." My father says as he exits the door.

"Okay, you guys, I figured we could hang out in my room if that's cool?"

"Yes, but of course, and don't think I forgot Yohan, I am totally dying to see your drawings."

"Oh my Gosh, me too."

We make our way to my room. I grab my sketchbook from off my table, hand it to Ella, and we all grab seats on the floor. That seems to be our thing.

"Wow, these are so cool, Yohan,"

"Oh my gosh, let me see."

"Wow, look at the detail on these. Yo-Yo, you are so talented. How are you single?"

"Girl, he might not be single for long, remember Nash?"

I'm turning red. I know it. I can't help it.

"Oh yeah, have you heard from him?" Lexie says, now flipping through pages in my sketchbook.

"No, not yet, but it's ok. I still haven't had time to do that sketch for him anyway, and it's looking like I might not get to it. Besides, I'll be leaving soon, and I really don't want anything long-distance, I mean, if he even likes me."

"Hey, who said you had to date him? A little fun never hurt anybody." Ella says with a wink.

"Okay, so we need to get down to business, but before that, can we, like, order a pizza or something? I'm beyond famished."

"Yeah, me too, and we are totally not doing Eat Your Heart Out Bakery for a while because obviously Patra's gone off the deep end."

"Okay, pepperoni good?" I suggest.

"I'm cool with that."

"Me too."

I order the pizza, Lexie and Ella power off their phones, and I stick mine under my pillow for good measure. I'm unsure if it'll make a difference, but I can't really power it off if we're expecting a delivery.

It's not long before Lexie offers up some entertainment by standing up and taking center stage in the middle of my room, her hairbrush in hand, which is now acting as a microphone as she pretends to host a television show that apparently, we are the stars of.

"Okay, tonight on Haus of Ascension, Madison faces her defeat, but how will they do it? Watch as these three friends devise the ultimate plan to take down the most treacherous tech villain known to mankind, Madison, whatever the hell her last name is!"

"Down with the demon!"

"Off with her head!"

We laugh, and though I am having fun, the severity of it all clicks back instantaneously, "Okay, you guys seriously, though, what are we thinking?"

"Well, I don't have a plan per se, but I brought my cards."

"Oh my God, yes, yes, why didn't we do this the other night?" Lexie asks gleefully as she reclaims her seat on the floor.

"I don't know, there was just so much going on already that I didn't really think of it, and you know it was supposed to be magic-free, just a fun night."

"True."

"Yeah, I mean, we did kind of say that."

She pulls her tarot cards out of her bag, and I swear I can feel this energy just emanating from them. They look so interesting, a gold color with intricate patterns of what I assume to be flowers decorating the backs.

"So, how does this work?"

"Well, I'm not that advanced of a reader, so I usually just do a three-card pull for past, present, and future to see how things are expected to go based on the energy we are vibrating in at the moment, but seeing as how I have a newfound gift, I was thinking maybe I just go with the flow."

"Do it, do it," Lexie chants, and I join in. "Yes, do it!"

She closes her eyes and begins to lay the cards on the floor.

One, two, three.

She stops.

"Hey, I thought you said you were going to use your intuition and go with the flow or whatever. I think we should do more like I've seen people do spreads in clips and stuff before."

"Yeah, I was thinking that too, Lex, but it's weird. I just feel like I should stop. I don't even feel like I should do it at all anymore. Something's telling me not to."

"Girl, then don't! If you don't pick those things off the floor and put them back in your bag."

"Yeah, you're right. We don't need tarot."

Before she can put the cards back in her bag, something comes over me. It's as if I'm being moved by a force, something out of my body, something that's not completely me, not my choice.

I reach over and flip the cards over, one by one.

Death, Death, Death.

"Oh, hell no," Lexie yells as she backs up from our circle.

"Oh my God, Yohan."

"How did I get all three death cards? What is the probability of that, Aella?"

"Unlikely, very unlikely, especially seeing as how there's only one death card in the deck."

I can't help but stand and pace around the room. I'm scared, and I'm sweating. I feel like I keep being told I'm going to die over and over again, and why me?

"It's just tarot, Yohan, and it's to be taken lightly. That's what the readers say. Besides, the future can always be changed, even if it is real. Let me just put these away."

She reaches for the three death cards that are now staring at me from the center of my room, and as she does, the deck spills from her lap, causing additional cards to land face up.

Death, Death, Death, Death.

"Put those damn things away now, Ella! No one is dying," Lexie screams as she attempts to unscrew the bottom of her hairbrush and takes a huge gulp of whiskey.

If I wasn't scared before, I am now. I am terrified.

Ring Ring

We all jump at the sound of my phone ringing from underneath my pillow. My first instinct is to ignore it, but then I remember... the pizza.

Thank God, something normal.

I answer the phone, tell the driver I am on my way, and let Lex and Ella know I will be right back up with our order. Hopefully, with some food in our system, we can reconvene and focus on an actual plan to get this whole Madison issue taken care of.

I meet the delivery driver at the front entrance, pay him, and make my way back up to my apartment while clumsily trying to stick my card back in my pocket. I have a habit of losing things, and with the way my luck is going so far, the last thing I need is to lose my bank card.

Just as I am about to enter the door, I hear a familiar voice calling my name.

"Yo-Yo, hey, what's up?"

I turn around and realize it's Nash.

Crap, I totally don't have that sketch done.

"Hey Nash, how's it going?"

"Good, good." He laughs. "That's a lot of pizza. Either you're having a party without me, or you're starving."

I redden.

This is your chance, Yohan, and you have your friends here, your wingmen or wing women or whatever.

Do it, ask him.

"Not really a party, just have some friends over. I mean, if you're not busy, you're welcome to join."

"I'd love to." He smirks.

Oh God, he's doing it again.

He's bewitching me.

We make our way into my apartment, and I set the pizzas down on the counter, look for plates and glasses so we can eat, and I can introduce the girls to Nash, but I am so nervous.

I hope they like him, and I am also really hoping they don't ask questions that will put me on the spot because I am already a nervous wreck.

"So, how's that sketch coming along?" he asks, now leaning on my counter and tussling his hair.

"To be honest, Nash, I'm really sorry, I haven't had a chance to start it yet. I just kind of been a little busy." I blurt out nervously.

He leans up off the counter and makes his way towards me.

Oh gosh, what is he doing?

"It's okay, Yohan, you want to know something funny?" he asks, moving closer.

"Uh, sure." I feel my chest tighten, and my heart is beating faster.

"I only asked for that sketch because I wanted a reason to talk to you." He licks his lips and continues to inch in closer. There's still a lot of space, but in my mind, we're only so far apart.

I'm dying, yea, I'm dying. This is what the cards were talking about. I'm getting warm.

Too warm.

"Oh, yeah?" I reply, voice shaky.

"Yeah, but we're running out of time. You're leaving, right?" he moves in closer.

"Y-yes, B-but we can keep in touch if you want?"

What is he doing?

He moves in closer, and we are only inches apart.

"I see the way you look at me, Yohan. You want me just as much as I want you. We have now. Let's use the time we have wisely and not wonder what if."

That's it, I'm going for it.

"Y-your right, but I'm nervous. I never really..."

"Yohan, who are you talking to?" I look over to find Ella looking at me strangely, with a look of concern, almost alarmed.

Nash turns his head, smiles, and offers up a wave to greet Ella.

I'm so rude.

Here I am in my kitchen, swooning and leaving my friends in my room without even introducing them.

I try to calm myself down. "Sorry, Ella, hey, this is Nash, the guy I was telling you about, the one I am working on the sketch for."

"What?" she makes her way into the kitchen.

"Nash, you know?" I repeat.

"Yohan..."

She looks from side to side and then back at me.

"There's no one here."

Chapter Sixteen

Yohan

"W-what? he's right here."

I feel my chest tighten and my breath speed up.

What is she talking about?

Can she really not see him?

"Lexie! Get in here." Ella screeches, voice shaky and in panic.

"She's right, you know."

I direct my attention back to Nash, who is now inching in closer, his smile twisting into something sinister, no longer friendly and inviting, no longer heroic.

"What?"

"They can't see me because I'm not real, Yohan. You know, you should really read more carefully if you're going to be playing with the unknown." He chuckles.

Read more carefully?

I watch as he looks me up and down, judging me. I can feel it. It's a feeling so familiar to me, something I feel anytime I walk out into the world: judged.

Judged for being different. Judged for being vulnerable. Judged for being me.

"Yes, Yohan, read more carefully. I am part of your world. I'm part of your thoughts. I am part of you, or what you desire, at least."

"Can you see it now? The desire to have your art appreciated. The desire to find someone who loves you, who shares similarities but offers up just a bit of something different? The desire to be sought out? To feel important?"

"I, Yohan, am your delusion."

My mind races back to the pages I've studied that Lexie sent over in the screenshots, the warnings, the heat-related effects, the mention of death, and this foreshadowed moment.

Nash, my permanent delusion.

"What's going on, Yohan? Why are you talking to yourself?" I can hear the panic in Lexie's voice; it's almost identical to the concern Ella has been projecting ever since she walked into the kitchen, but I can't respond, even though I know they're there.

It's Nash.

I am entirely focused on Nash.

"It's okay, Yohan, you know, to be delusional."

"To think you're worthy of love, and after all this time, it would mysteriously pop up into your life because of some random pages of what you consider to be magic has been guiding you blindly through decisions, decisions you have been too weak to make on your own."

"The truth is, you never even try. You're always too scared to take a chance. You never even tried to call or seek me out on your own. I only pop up when you're lonely."

He grimaces. "Poor pathetic you."

"Ever wonder why my number wasn't there when you only got enough confidence to try to contact me when your friends told you to? Or why my name is so similar to the boy you've been trying to save? The one you're afraid you might have feelings for?"

"Because I am not real; I am just as inauthentic as the creatures you design."

"Wake up, Yohan, life is not a fairytale!"

"SHUT UP!"

He inches closer, closing the gap that was barely even present between us, and an abundance of emotions flood over me.

I can feel his breath, and it's enchanting.

How can I still desire something that clearly wants to hurt me?

How can I want something that I know is not real?

He lifts his shirt to reveal his tattoo, and my eyes can't help but survey his skin.

"Your black rose? Am I what you desire? Your dream love come to fruition?"

"How embarrassing." He laughs.

"You can muster up something a little more creative than that, can't you?"

"Yohan! I don't know what's happening or what Madison is doing to you, but you need to use the spiral!" I can hear Lexie, which aids in breaking my daze, but if she only knew, this isn't Madison. This is a battle with myself, a creation of my very own insecurities manifested in real time.

"Yohan, you wouldn't want me to go, would you? I can still be yours; they can't see me, but you can. You can feel me. The touch was real. Look at me, Yohan."

I can't help but gaze into his eyes; the magic that lies behind them is so powerful. Everything I ever wanted, and it's calling me, his essence, his everything.

He was meant for me.

He is mine.

"Yes, desire me, Yohan, give in to me, and you can be free, free from all of this. The world will no longer judge you, and you will no longer feel alone. Give in to me, Yohan."

I can't help but succumb to his will.

I am melting.

This is what I want; this is what I need.

I close my eyes and lean into my instinct to experience my delusion, to feel that sensation I desire, to get that one kiss, the kiss I know might end me, but I don't care.

"Even more pathetic than I thought." His voice is now rough, angry, and menacing.

I feel a grip around my throat, and I am lunged into the wall behind me, lifted up off the ground, and enveloped in panic.

"Oh my God, my vision, Lexie. What do we do?"

"The spiral, Yohan! Focus, use the spiral!"

I feel his grip tighten as he laughs and feeds off my fear. I try to close my eyes and focus.

I need you to work for me this time.

I need you to work NOW!

He tightens his grip, and my airway is closing; I am holding on. I won't be defeated, especially not by him, by me.

Focus on the center of the Spiral.

Spin, Spiral, Spin.

My intent is to destroy him.

My intent is to keep him from hurting me.

Ignite for me, spiral!

The flame dances at the spiral's end, just as it always does, but nothing is happening.

This can't be it. This can't be how it ends.

"What a sad excuse for a supposed witch, ha-ha, and you really thought you were chosen? What an obvious clerical mistake."

"As I said before, you are pathetic." He squeezes my throat even harder.

As I'm fighting for air, it clicks what he said before…

That I should have read more carefully.

What am I missing?

The thoughts come rushing in as if by magic.

Charge it with your essence. Make it yours.

The warning.

Words have power.

I can hear both Ella and Lexie expressing concern and trying to figure out a way to help me in the background. I know there isn't much they can do, but just having them here for me at this moment gives me the boost I need.

"Just give in already. Let yourself be free." Nash snarls.

"You call me pathetic, but at least I am real. I exist." I snap back.

I feel the anger rise in me in a way I never felt before, and this time, I am entirely focused.

I think about the spiral in a completely different way.

I think about it as if it is constructed using little bits and pieces of me, of the things I hold important, the things I value most.

I now envision the jagged little meaningless lines that once created the spiral as words that have meaning to me, words that hold power.

Art, Magic, Perseverance, Love, Strength.

The things that kept me going when I thought all I wanted to do was give up.

I close my eyelids down even harder and see my spiral take form, the words all connecting to create a spiral that is truly mine and no longer generic.

The spiral glows red.

He tightens his grip on my throat, and just as my vision begins to go black, a sensation of falling is taking over my entire body.

I fall into my thoughts.

My intent is to destroy him.

Spin for me, spiral, spin.

I see the spiral spin and pick up speed, making me dizzy.

Ignite for me, spiral!

The flame that only ever danced at the end of the spiral engulfs the words, slowly but picking up pace, setting them all aflame.

Art, Magic, Perseverance, Love, Strength.

I grow unbearably hot; the heat building up in my chest intensely, burning, flaring, scorching until it finally exits my body through my chest, and all I can see is black.

I no longer feel the grip around my throat, and I am gasping for air, desperately trying to bring myself back to reality, back from this internal battle.

"Oh my God, Yohan! Are you okay?"

As I regain consciousness, I notice Lexie and Ella hovering over me in my kitchen, and I can't help but let the tears flow freely. That was so much emotion, and I'm tired of holding it all in.

"It's okay, Yohan, we got you," Lexie says as she takes a seat next to me on my kitchen floor.

"We're a team, Haus of Ascension, remember?" Ella says, now joining me and Lexie.

I try to pull myself together and wipe away the tears. "You know, I think you were right, Lex. This is all my fault. The thing I was battling, my delusion, said I was too pathetic to go for the things I wanted, and that's why I was chasing magic, living in a dream. This is all happening because of me."

"Get it together, Yohan. You are anything but pathetic, you are unique, and that's why we like you. It takes more strength to stand up and be yourself than to sit down and blend in, and if you ask me, you are doing a damn good job."

"I agree with Lex on this one, Yo-Yo. We're all a bit different, but that's what got us all here in the first place. It wasn't you. It's us, and we will conquer this as a team now. Pull yourself together. We've got friends to save and a tech witch to vanquish!"

"Still with that vanquishing thing?"

"Yeah, I like the sound of it."

"I do, too," I add, chuckling.

"Well, let's vanquish her ass, then!" Lexie adds as they both help me up, and I shake off all the leftover feeling of defeat that is lingering within me.

"On a side note, that spiral, Yohan! That was some intense shit! That thing came flying across the room. Me and Lex jumped out the way like, whoa."

"Was it? I couldn't see what was happening; I only saw it in my mind."

"Yes, it was, and now that you know how to project it, we can definitely take Madison down. How did you do it?"

"Well, my delusion told me I should've paid more attention to the pages, so I thought about the words and made the spiral my own. I was missing that before. I just thought of it as geometric lines like my tattoo."

"Smart, see, and you call yourself pathetic. Well, if that is pathetic, I want to be pathetic too."

"Okay, you guys, one last thing on the checklist before we take on Madison. Yohan, can you pull up that video of Bash?"

Crap.

I'm such a bad friend. I'm so caught up in thinking of myself and all my issues that I keep forgetting that Bash is literally hoping that I find a way to save him.

Don't worry, Bash, I'm coming, and now I have something in my back pocket.

This time, I'm saving you.

We make our way to my room; I grab my laptop, prop it open, and click the file I saved from my V-Messenger.

As we try to pick the video apart, freezing frame by frame, it doesn't seem to have any new clues or anything too telling that would give us an upper hand or any advantage while walking into this, so we decide to just call it quits.

"Well, I guess we're going in blind," Lexie states, now titling her hairbrush above her head, trying to grab the last drops of whiskey.

"Not completely. We know these queens are using magic and trying to harvest energy, so that's a plus. We just don't know why, and why drag queens, that seems pretty random."

"None of this makes sense, really," I state, now reaching for my Cannapuffy to help keep my anxiety under control.

"True, so you guys ready to get Madison out of our hair once and for all?"

"If there was ever a time, it's now. I'm full of whiskey and ready for battle!"

"Let's do this!" I exclaim, reaching my fist into the center of our circle.

"Haus of Ascension, operation vanquish her initiated," Ella says, now connecting her fist.

"I'll show her what happens when you call me a hoe." Lexie roars as she adds her fist to the circle.

We all laugh and make our way to my door, ready for whatever the rest of the night will bring.

It can't get any worse, and even if it does, we've got this.

We were meant for this.

None of this is a coincidence.

We were destined to walk this path.

It's magic.

It's fated.

Lexie

WHAT THE HELL JUST happened?

His delusion?

"It's now or never, you guys, Haus of Ascension vs. Aggy Maddie."

My thought process is disrupted by Ella's attempt to add some confidence to our egos as we walk towards Eat Your Heart Out Bakery to check to see if Quinn and Reggie left any information that might help us take Madison down.

At least we know he can project the spiral. That's one thing we have on our side, and Quinn and Reggie also said our protection wish must have worked sooo...

"I know this probably isn't the right timing, seeing as how we're on our way to have this battle with Madison and whatnot, but I've had something on my mind I've been wanting to ask you guys."

I look at her, then Yohan, and take a deep breath, anticipating what might come next. We have so much on our plates right now that another layer of problems will be anything other than beneficial.

She continues.

"So, I think we had a great time the other night, aside from Madison's text message harassment, of course, so I was thinking, Lexie, you've been looking to get your own place, right?"

I totally know where she is going with this, and I am so one hundred percent in.

"Yes, I need space, girl," I respond confidently to let her know I am serious.

"And Yohan, you mentioned you wanted to stay here, but your dads moving, so I was thinking, with my brothers out and two extra rooms, we could all split rent, and it totally makes sense to stick together as much as possible seeing as how were not sure how this whole magic thing is going to play out."

I look over to Yohan and see a smile illuminate his face. It's so refreshing to see because after what happened in that kitchen with his delusion, he seemed so sullen.

"I would love that. I don't know how my dad will take it, but I'm tired of picking everything up and starting all over. Plus, I've never felt more at home than here with you guys. There's something about this place that makes me know this is all meant to be."

"So, it's settled then. Haus of Ascension is literally becoming the house of Ascension."

I can't help but laugh. "Ella, you really are taking this thing too far now."

We continue our walk to Eat Your Heart Out Bakery while we discuss room arrangements, updating décor, and taking advantage of our employee discounts, compliments of FURNISH.

I'm a girl who loves to shop, so I'm already decorating everything in my mind, from peel-and-stick wallpaper to the bedding and rug options. I'm creating a space that will dazzle any onlooker once complete.

When we finally arrive at Eat Your Heart Out Bakery, the place seems jam-packed from the outside tonight. It's a good thing we're not going in to eat and we're just making a quick stop to check for the note.

"What is she doing over there?" Yohan asks, and that's when I notice Patra leaning up against the side of the gargoyle, puffing smoke as usual, but this time, she's holding something, something that belongs to us.

"Hey Patra, how's it..."

She interrupts.

"I thought I made it clear, Lexie. I said I see everything, and when I see things going left, people are uninvited."

She holds the torn envelope in the air.

"What is this? And why are you using my place of business to send messages? There are quicker tools used for communication in this day and age. I demand an explanation."

Ella steps forward.

"We don't owe you any damn explanation, Patra. We've been your patrons for some time now. We've been loyal, and just in case you didn't notice, you're not the only bar in town."

"Aella, you're usually timid. I must say your new attitude is shocking but needs adjustment. It doesn't quite work for you. I can clearly tell Miss Lexie here is the leader of the pack, so once again, Lexie, I ask you, what is this?"

She removes the paper from the envelope and reads its contents.

"Remember, work together. The energy is there."

Work together?

I quickly move my train of thought back to how to rectify the situation currently happening between the three of us and Patra. Though Yohan is primarily quiet, I'm hoping he's not trying to conjure the spiral because clearly, there's nothing magical about Patra unless the ability to be annoyingly intrusive now counts as whimsical.

I come up with a quick lie to hopefully satiate her need for answers.

"It's just a game we're playing with friends, sort of like a scavenger hunt. We leave notes at our favorite places as clues to find items, you know, keeps us off our devices and lets us experience the real world."

Damn, I'm a good liar. Maybe I should become a lawyer.

"I see, I like that, and here I am thinking you guys are planning on doing something to my bar. I've worked hard for the place, you know." She smiles and hands the letter to me.

"I'd love to be a part of this little game you guys have going. Let me know if there's anything I can do to help." She winks and makes her way inside the bakery.

"Creepy as hell." Yohan finally breaks his silence.

"Yeah, but let's forget about her for now. What do they mean by working together? Aren't we already doing that?" I ask them both, hoping they can pick up on something I may have been missing.

"Well, have either of you tried to project the spiral? I'm thinking other than the wishing spell, it's all we have, and maybe it's not just meant for me."

"I haven't," I answer quickly, and Ella's same response immediately follows.

"Well, now that I've experienced the full weight of it, I can give you some hints. The key is to make the spiral personal, constructed of things that matter most to you. For me, it was art. You have to look at the things that keep you going and construct the spiral from there. It can't hurt to try."

He's right; it's all we have, and we need to go in with something. If the note's a hint, this must be what Quinn and Reggie are referring to.

"Okay, got it. We can memorize the basics of the spiral on the way there. I've ordered a Dryve, and it says it should be here in ten minutes. I hope you guys are ready because I'm ready, but I'm also terrified."

I have to agree with Ella. I am terrified, too, not necessarily of Madison but more so of what she is capable of. It's true what they say: knowledge is power, and if she claims to know as much as she does, we could be done for.

"Let's not be nervous, you guys. I did it. I projected the spiral. Let's focus on that. If I can do it, I know you guys can, too. We're a team, remember, and one thing is for sure, we're not going down without a fight. We might be a group of misfits, but we're not to be fucked with."

I don't know where that little speech came from in Yohan, but I am living for it.

"You're right. Let's do this." Just as my confidence rises back up, I notice our Dryve pulling up. I don't know about Yo-Yo and Ella, but my adrenaline is pumping through the roof right now, and I cannot wait to finish this girl off once and for all.

The Dryve ride is so quiet I swear you can hear a pin drop. Our faces are buried in our phones, studying the spiral and trying to memorize every last word to make sure we get this right. This is our only shot, and we have to succeed.

When our driver finally pulls up to Ellington Park, we all exit the car and pretend to walk past the entrance just in case he is still looking since, technically, we are trespassing because it's after operating hours.

Ella points out an opening in the fence, which we make our way through and begin walking through the dark park using only our flashlights from our phones as a light source.

"Yeah, maybe we should've thought this out better. I mean, meeting our arch nemesis in a large park in the middle of the night without a specific meeting point doesn't seem like the smartest idea."

"I concur." Yohan agrees while he drags his feet annoyingly through the leaves of Ellington Park.

A total pet peeve of mine. Please pick those feet up.

I look to the left and notice three more lights shining, and instantly, I know it's them, Quinn, Reggie, and her evil Madison.

My heart starts to race.

"Okay, that must be them over there," I state, trying to keep my voice as calm as possible. If I'm supposed to be a leader, I cannot show fear. I'm not allowed to.

We make our way over to them, and as I take Madison in, she's not as I expected. She's shorter, dressed a bit sloppier than I anticipated, and her demeanor less confident than on screen. Talk about the right angles and the magic of filters.

"Hey, bitches, nice to see you in person for once." She giggles, and it's annoying. That hasn't changed.

"Wish we could say the same," I respond before throwing a quick look at Reggie and Quinn, who are standing awkwardly quiet behind her.

"So, I ask my loves one last time, are you going to will me these pages or not? It will make things... simpler, and simple is what you want unless you want messy. I can do either-or honey, it doesn't take much, like a flick of a switch, ya know?"

"Shove the switch up your ass, Madison!" Ella yells, which I admit takes me by surprise.

"So messy it is, then." She turns her back to us and Quinn and Reggie quickly follow suit.

I am instinctively feeling the urge to lunge at her, but I know better. This isn't her first rodeo, and I will not give her the satisfaction of defeating me.

I hear her rustling through what I assume is her hot pink fanny pack I noticed around her waist earlier.

Just as Ella, Yohan, and I have enough time to share a look of confusion, the three of them turn back to face us, but this time, they are all wearing masks, and Madison, their self-proclaimed leader, is now wielding what seems to be a pink glittery perfume bottle in her hand.

She sprays exactly three sprays into the night air.

WTF

She begins to speak, her voice muffled by her hot pink mask.

"You like it? It's one of my little secret creations. I'm a bit of a scent connoisseur, a mixologist, if you will." She giggles.

"I call this one... Gotcha Bitch. Isn't it literally stunning?" She makes her way toward us, and I suddenly realize I cannot move. I cannot speak.

I am frozen in place.

She walks circles around the three of us in what I assume is her attempt to taunt us and piss us off while we're frozen in place, basically helpless.

"You know, I played this as kindly as possible. I asked nicely. I did little things, but nothing big. I didn't release your pictures, Yohan, but now, seeing as how I have to do extra work, I just might..."

"...I mean, unless I kill you all by mistake, then there's no point, really. I prefer torture. I find it more satisfying."

UGHHHH

I literally want to pound her face in.

"Okay, but enough wasting time. I was joking. I won't be killing you by mistake. It will be intentional, ha-ha."

My blood is boiling as I watch her take her place back in front of Reggie and Quinn, who are doing absolutely nothing to help. How could we trust them? What was the point of all that?

She reaches into her pocket, unlocks her phone, and points it towards us. "Sudo Su." She screeches.

Just as the words escape her mouth, I cannot believe what I am seeing. A digital string of what looks like cryptic text or code comes flooding out of her phone in real time and surrounds us, dragging us helplessly across the dirt and pinning us to the elm tree behind us, tightening its grip as the seconds pass by.

She looks at Quinn and giggles. "I don't even know what Sudo Su means, ha ha."

Quinn speaks for the first time. "It's a technical command used for…"

"Oh my God, Quinn, shut up. No one cares. It's not funny anymore if you have to explain it."

I notice the annoyance on Quinn's face. Maybe not all hope is lost after all.

"Regretting not willing me the pages now, huh? Helpless little Lexie?"

I still cannot move, but I manage to spit, and I hope my message is sent.

"Oh, not going quick enough for you? I can fix that." She points her phone at us once again.

"Sudo Su, tighten."

The digital string tightens, and I feel the air lessening and the pain increasing.

I look over to my friends, who seem to be in just as much agony as me, but I notice Yohan's eyes are closed, and I know what he is doing.

He is calling his spiral.

I dart my eyes towards Ella, then Yo-Yo, hoping she gets my mental message, and just like that, she closes her eyes as well, and I know we are on the same page.

My eyes close, and I hear two familiar voices fall in sync before I can start conjuring the spiral.

"Sudo Su, Sudo Su."

Quinn and Reggie.

Although my eyes are closed, it doesn't take long for me to realize they are using Madison's own tactics against her, holding her in place with the cryptic digital text string.

"Hurry, we can't hold her for long. She can escape it. The only thing stopping her is her focus on her own magic. You can do it, work fast!"

The desperation in Quinn's voice awakens the drive I need to push forward. Pain aside, I must conjure this spiral.

I think about what Yohan said, make the spiral personal, constructed of the things that matter most to me. I think of my family.

I envision the spiral being made from little photos of the memories I'll never forget, the ones with my sister, the ones with my parents, the ones with my new friends, the memories I can instantly go back to with the magic of music. I think of it all and watch my spiral take its shape and begin to glow red, flame dancing at the end, waiting to ignite.

Spin for me, Spiral, Spin.

My intent is to protect us.

Still Chapter Seventeen

(A)ella

*T**HE THINGS THAT ARE* *most important to me.*

I think of my designs, my desire to be appreciated, to not be the last one out, to matter just as much as my brothers.

I think of my spiral constructed of my ties, my wearable memories, each one paying homage to a certain point of my life, my wearable stories.

The ones I've created or received and how I put them all together for self-renewal. My magic lies in my ability to design.

I see my spiral take form and glow red, ready to ignite, and I watch the flame dance at its end.

Spin for me, Spiral, Spin.

My intent is to protect us.

Yohan

I BEGIN TO SUMMON the spiral, which is now growing so familiar to me that it comes at ease.

I construct the spiral of words that kept me going.

Art, Magic, Perseverance, Love, Strength.

It glows red.

I see the flame dancing at the end, and it feels like it's meant to be. The spiral is a part of who I am.

Spin for me, Spiral, Spin.

My intent is to protect us.

Nash

*H*E CANNOT DIE. *I am a part of him.*

I know the power used against me.

I am permanent as long as he lives. I cannot be destroyed.

His power is my power.

I am not only his delusion; I am his weapon.

His love has kept me alive.

I think of the things that are important to me.

It is him.

I am here to protect Yohan.

I think of his strength, how hard it must be to keep going, to keep pushing in a world where you feel like an outcast.

He is strong, and I am a part of him.

I use his words of power to construct my spiral.

I see the spiral take shape and begin to glow red.

The flame dances at the end.

My intention is to protect him.

Spin for me, Spiral, spin.

Haus of Ascension

Ignite for me, spiral.

Lexie

THE INTENSITY OF THE rush of heat forcefully making its way from my chest causes my eyes to quickly open with a sense of alarm, and I cannot believe what I am currently witnessing.

Four spirals rush towards Madison, knocking her to the ground, her phone falling quickly after her and shattering to pieces. I watch as the strings of text dissipate into thin air.

Four?

We are freed from our constriction to the elm tree, and something about Madison changes, first subtly, but then it picks up speed, and the Madison I've grown to know is no longer the girl lying in front of me.

She quickly scavenges through her fanny pack, clearly looking for something to save her from the effects of the spiral. She pulls another phone out of nowhere, points it towards us, and screams her words of power, "Sudo Su!".

The phone shatters instantly, just like the one before it, bursting shards of glass and plastic into her hand, which is now slowly trickling blood.

"Why have you forsaken me?" she screams into the air, voice desperate and withdrawn.

As I try to make sense of what I am seeing, a small tube rolls to my feet, similar to a glass tube of lip gloss... no wait, it is a small tube of lip gloss with a handwritten label displaying a single word: glamour.

I pick up the tube and stick it in my pocket. I'm smart enough to know it's something witchy, and it might come in handy at some point if we decide to continue down this path.

I try to decipher what's going on with Madison from a distance without getting too close. She's probably not out of tricks just yet, but all I can hear is her sobbing.

Her attention is not at all on us. We swap gazes and remain silent, trying to eavesdrop on bits and pieces of the conversation between her, Quinn, and Reggie.

"I trusted you guys. How could you?" she sniffles.

"Madison, we're not dumb. You were plotting against us. We would've never let you get killed, but you got power hungry. That's what this stuff can do to you."

Reggie attempts to console her by placing a hand on her shoulder, which is quickly swatted away.

"Listen, Lexie and her team aren't that bad. Maybe we can..."

"NEVER!" She screeches and attempts to stand, and that's when I fully notice the difference in her. She's older, and as the moonlight hits her, I see her blonde hair in patches. It is clearly not her natural hair color, and whatever enchantment she was under must have been disrupted by the spirals.

The differences in her from the Madison that has been stalking and threatening me are revealing themselves before my eyes. Her skin is not as radiant; I can see the bruises and marks on her flesh, and her body is telling a story completely different from the one she used her mouth to profess.

She directs her attention to me. "What, Lexie? Huh? Like you haven't used a few beauty tricks of your own, you don't know me, and I don't care what you think."

She turns back to her friends, "But you, Quinn, you do. You know what he did to me and how it was so important for me to find something to make me happy, this, the whole adventure, it was fulfilling, it was fun, it was an escape, and you took that from me."

He? What? Who did this to her? And what did they do?

"We don't want to..." Yohan attempts to make a statement, but Madison quickly brings it to a halt.

"I don't care what you want, Yo-Yo, and you, Lexie, you win."

"I will you my pages, all except for one."

"The one that was truly meant for me and only me."

"Have fun on your journey, and I'll see you at the end."

My phone pings, and I don't even need to check it. I know it's an email with Madison's pages. When she said he willed me her pages, I knew she meant it, not only because of the tears streaming down her face, but because I felt it. I felt something click, something I can't explain.

All except for one?

I try to wrap my head around why she would want to keep one page and how that would help her, seeing as how she wasn't satisfied with the several she already had, but before I can get any further into my thoughts, my questions are answered.

"I accept my fate!" she screams into the air, voice shrill and desperate.

"I eligere ad fontem redire. I choose to return to source". She drops to the ground, lifts her now blood-soaked hand to the sky, and slams it so hard to the ground I hear her wrist snap, which sends chills all the way through every part of my body.

I can hear the gasps from behind me as Yohan and Ella are taking in what is happening in front of the five of us right now.

I watch as Madison slowly turns to dust, returning to the earth as she requested.

It starts with her snapped wrist, changing color and blending into the tones of the ground below us. Her body quickly follows as she returns to source and becomes to us no more.

I can't help but look over at Quinn and Reggie, who are obviously holding their emotions in. No matter how bad someone treats you, it's hard to see them go. This is something I know deep in my heart, so I ache for their loss. A friend is a friend, whether they have negative qualities or not.

As if we're all in sync, maybe because of our shared spiral incantation, Yo-Yo, Ella, and I simultaneously attempt to make our way towards Quinn and Reggie, to offer condolences or remorse, to just be human, but we are stopped by Quinn's hand pushed forward signaling a halt.

"It had to be done." She states simply but effectively.

"Me and Reggie are going to go our own way. Paths are predetermined; we were meant to meet, and maybe we will find our paths crossing again in the future, but for now, we need distance."

"But we can work together." Ella offers up, her voice emotional and noticeably filled with regret.

"Yeah, we can put the pieces together and use what we know to find...."

Yohan is cut off.

"We will go our separate ways, and trying to find the source of this invitation to magic is pointless. Don't you think we've all tried?"

"It's just like life without magic. You keep going because you must, because it's all you know. This just comes with a different layer of problems, and me and Reggie here have enough problems of our own."

"We're out. If we cross, we'll be allies. Until then, goodnight."

I watch them walk away, and I don't know why, but it's painful. I barely know them, but it doesn't make it hurt any less.

All the events of the night continue to play through my mind as we make our exit out of the park. The walk is quiet and awkward, and none of us dare to muster up conversation. We are all drained, and it's not even over yet.

We still need to help Yohan's friend and save Ella's brothers.

Our Dryve approaches, and we make our way in.

As the Dryve continues down its path, dropping off Ella first, then Yohan, I get lost in my thoughts as usual.

Is this really as endless as Quinn made it seem?

Is this just a new way to live life?

There must be an answer somewhere.

Who thought of all this, and what is the point?

As the Dryve approaches my house, I have one last thought that I am determined to follow all the way through.

I will find whoever started all this no matter how long it takes, and they better hope I'm missing a few pages of this shit because I, Lexie Smith, am determined to go all the way in!

Chapter Eighteen

(A)ella

I can't believe it's over.

She's really gone.

Not just gone, she's dead.

It's not our fault, we didn't do this. She wanted to go.

It's impossible to wrap my head around all the events that have happened so quickly over the past few days.

I have to admit, not only has it been scary and challenging to navigate, but I'm also beginning to rethink my whole involvement in this little magical ordeal, and a part of me wishes things would just return to normal.

I try to shift my mind towards more positive thoughts and focus on the fact that my two best friends in the world right now are going to be moving in with me. I can finally brush away this feeling of loneliness that has been dwelling in this apartment ever since my brothers went on their hunt for fame.

As I make my way through the apartment, cleaning and preparing my brother's old rooms for Lexie and Yohan, I can't help but think that this is far from over.

Although I am still angry at Aeden and Asher for abandoning me and not considering my feelings before abruptly picking up and moving to a brand-new city, I do miss them. I will still do anything to protect them, even if, to them, I remain just an afterthought.

I pack up the things that they left behind in their rooms into boxes and store them in the closet just in case they need them in the future.

I know they're on a new journey, but it doesn't mean I won't ever see them again. I mean, we're literally going to see them tonight after work when we head to Bixie's.

Crap, that's what I forgot.

I close the closet door, locking my brothers' left-behind belongings away for safekeeping and make my way to my laptop.

I pry it open and hit the search engines, typing in a query for Bixie's Live Drag Battle and how to get tickets.

The replies come in quickly, and I already knew that the show was filmed over in Fairview because they mentioned that before they left. My primary concern is how to get in, and with no response to the several text messages I have been sending, the internet is my only resource for information at the moment.

The price points on the tickets are pretty high, and even if we could afford them, we should have already purchased them because every ticket site I navigate to shows that they are completely sold out.

Damnit, what do we do now?

Magic?

Sneak in?

I'm definitely going to need Lexie and Yo-Yo's help on this one because there is no way we are waiting any longer to make sure my brothers are safe, and I'm pretty sure Yohan will agree when it comes to saving his friend Bash, who is obviously in trouble according to the video, we've all tried to make sense of.

Feeling deflated, I close my laptop and proceed to get ready for work. I still have a bit of time and consider consulting my cards for some insight on what we should do next, but then I quickly remember my last run-in with tarot and decide that it's probably not the best idea.

Once I'm dressed, I double-check for my badge, take one last look around my apartment to ensure it's up to standards for my new room-mates, and make my way to the door, where I take a seat and wait for my Dryve.

The Dryve arrives rather quickly. I make my way in, say hello to the driver, and get lost in my phone.

I scroll through social media and look at people having regular lives, which makes me miss the mundane, the things I took for granted.

When the Dryve finally arrives at the *Torture Chamber,* I hesitate a bit before I open the car door, thank Gus, my driver, and grab my things from the back of his car, and proceed to sloppily drag my feet to the store entrance.

I scan myself in and reluctantly head to Bedrooms, my new department for the week.

I pray for any creeper who decides to throw one of their advances at me today because with the week I've been having, I might just launch a spiral at their ass and put them in their place.

The store is pretty dead today, and Bedrooms is no different. I spend most of my time fixing the bedding, reorganizing the displays laid across the side tables, and laying color swatches for customers to see all the available options we have for the pieces we offer.

It's not long before the boredom settles in.

I miss working directly with Yo-Yo and Lexie. It's something about working with the people you vibe with that really makes the day go by.

I take a seat on one of the king-size beds, the one currently decorated with my favorite comforter, a deep lavender with a gold accent, and whip out my phone to send a text to the grouper.

> Hey guys, lunch at our usual spot today?

The replies come in quickly.

> Yes, I would think a few days with Rose, and I'd get used to her, but no, she's still annoying.

> Yes, we need to talk about our plans for tonight and also the new pages. I think I have an idea!

> Okay, sounds....

Just as I'm typing my reply, I hear a voice behind me.

"Why is it that no one follows the simple rule of no phones on the sales floor?"

It's Jaden, recently promoted Jaden, here to flex his bit of power.

"There are literally no customers here, Jaden. It was just a quick text."

He shakes his head from side to side and sighs, "Rules are rules, Aella. I'm sorry, but I'm going to have to issue you a write-up. If this is the only way to make sure our customers are getting the attention they deserve, it must be done."

"Jaden, what customers!?" I snap.

"Now, Ella, let's not take this beyond where it needs to go. I'll call you into the office later to go over the paperwork, but for now, please stay off of your phone."

I offer a stiff smile and wait for him to walk away.

I swear to God, he better hope there's nothing in these new pages I'll be tempted to use on him because now he is just asking for it.

He turns his head as he makes his way out of Bedrooms and into the marketplace.

"Nice tie, by the way." He winks.

He is really asking for it.

I have no choice but to try to power through the first half of my workday, even though I feel completely drained, and the lack of customers and social interaction, in general, is just making it worse.

I manage to get through the lag, and eventually, break time rolls around. I'm hoping whatever Lexie has found will help boost my mood and give me the energy I so desperately need.

I make my way to our meeting spot by the smoker's area to find Lexie and Yohan already seated and in a full-blown discussion of what I assume is a review of what exactly happened the night prior with the whole Madison confrontation and her dramatic demise.

I grab a seat and quickly find out I am right.

"I mean, I didn't like her but to see her so depleted and then to turn to literal dust like that? It was scary. What does that mean for us?"

"Hey guys,"

"Hey, Ella, girl, I have some things to tell you guys now that we're all here."

"Yeah, I've been dying to know what's on these new pages, not to mention we need a plan before we just head to Bixie's."

Lexie offers a smile excitedly but also a bit devious, which sends a sense of excitement rushing through my body because when this girl has an idea, it's usually epic.

"Well, first things first, the new pages. I set something up for us. I barely got any sleep, but I figured if we have one more major task at hand, preparation is definitely necessary."

I see the curiosity peak in Yohan's eyes, and I'm starting to see what Lexie means about his fascination with magic.

"Are either of you familiar with DocDrive?"

"Like the online file-sharing service?" Yohan quickly answers.

"Yes, exactly."

"I've heard of it but never needed to use it for anything."

"Same."

She hands us sheets of pink paper with an access code.

"Okay, well, get ready to become familiar with their platform because I've created a shared document for us, something like a digital book of shadows or, if we're talking old school, like an online grimoire."

"I thought it made more sense if we could always have access to the pages, not need to look through text threads, and along the way, it would be easier to add anything new we find, and we can all update and edit as we go along."

"I did password protect it, which is what the access codes are for, but if what we know so far is true, if the pages aren't meant for an individual or willed by us, there shouldn't be much to worry about."

"Oh my God, I love that. It's genius!" I exclaim.

"Right?" She does her signature hair flip and leans in.

"But that's not all. I also have a plan to take on these queens."

Yohan leans in closer, which prompts me to follow suit, although I have no idea why we're acting as if we're sharing an enormous secret when there is absolutely no one around.

"Spill, girl, Spill."

"Well, the other night, Madison dropped this."

She pulls what looks like a small tube of lip gloss from her pocket.

"Lip Gloss?" Yohan asks, looking completely lost.

"Yes, lip gloss. When she dropped it, I knew it was something magical, but it wasn't until I was going through the new pages that I discovered how magical it really was."

"Well, what does it do besides make your lips shiny?"

She chuckles.

"Well, according to the pages, it's used for what's called a glamour."

"A glamour?"

"So, a glamour basically lets you present yourself to people in a way of your choosing, like a disguise is the best way I can describe it, but it also affects your personality too, which is why the Madison we saw once the spiral broke her glamour was not the Madison we were used to."

"Okay, I get it, I think, but how are we going to use it?"

"Well, you guys," she looks at me and then at Yohan.

"Get ready to get absolutely sickening, Hunty's, because we are becoming drag queens!"

Oh my God, slash, Goddess.

"Yaass!" I can hardly contain my excitement. If there's one thing I love, it is fashion, and in the drag world, they know fashion.

"So yeah, I'm open-minded, but drag? That's a bit much for me."

I scoot closer to Yohan. I have to remind him of the bigger picture: why we are really doing this.

"Think about Bash. I know you want to save him, and besides, this might be fun. Look at all the things you've done so far that you thought you couldn't. This is just one more thing to add to that bad-ass magical resume."

I nudge him for encouragement.

"Just think, Yohan, how cool it would be for you to save him this way, a hero in makeup, the thing he loves."

Lexie has a point. It's kind of poetic.

He swaps his look of worry for a grin, and I know we've said the right things.

"Okay, I'm in, but if I look like an idiot, count on payback in the future."

"Yay, so moving on, next on the list," Lexie directs her attention to me.

"You miss Ella without the A. Have you had any visions? Have you seen anything in your cards that can help?"

"I honestly have been scared to touch the cards since my deck went all mind of its own last time, and I've only had that one vision about Yohan and his delusion."

"Well, maybe we can trigger it. Think about it. Did anything specific happen when you had your last vision? Anything that might have prompted it?"

I begin to rustle through my thoughts.

It was the night my brothers told me they were moving. I had been crying. I was making my skirt.

That's it, the construction of the skirt.

The prick of the needle.

"I was making that skirt I wore with all the ties I was sewing, and I pricked my finger. I think it might've been triggered by the pain or shock or something?"

Yohan chimes in, "That sounds about right, most times..."

Smack

I grab my face. "Lexie, what the fuck!"

"No? Nothing? I'm just saying, girl, we don't have much time. I had to try something."

"Yohan, you try. Your hands are bigger."

I stand up. "Absolutely not! Yo-Yo, don't you dare!"

"I wouldn't, Ella, don't worry."

I reclaim my seat, rubbing my face and make sure to toss Lexie an evil glare.

"Well, do you have a needle on you? Maybe try pricking your finger." Yohan suggests.

"I don't, but thank you, Yohan. Your idea was way more reasonable than Lexie's over here."

"Girl, if we're going to be witches, you need to toughen up. I mean, we literally just saw Madison basically turn to dust. All I did was smack you."

"Fair... I guess."

I continue to rub my face to ease the sting from Lexie's surprise attack.

"So, magic aside for a sec, I've got the place ready for you guys, so whenever you want to start bringing stuff over, you can."

"I figured we'd meet after work at my place, and we can catch the train over to Fairview. If we get the four o'clock, we should be there a little after the show starts."

"Sounds good. I'm only bringing little things. I don't have much, and girl, they work us to death in this place, so I'm taking advantage of the discount and getting some new shit, okay?"

"Yeah, I don't have much either, mainly my art supplies, and I'm with Lexie on this one. I think I'll get some stuff delivered from FURNISH, too. It just seems easier."

"Aw man, you guys are making me want new stuff."

"Well, do it, girl, it's the new you remember? We're on a new adventure might as well start fresh."

"Yes, I agree," Yohan adds.

ping

I peer down at my phone and swipe away the daily affirmation notification.

"Crap, we've been talking so long we're fifteen minutes over break time."

"Shit."

"Damnit, Jaden's going to bitch."

"Yeah, he said he was going to write me up earlier. Talk about a power trip, like remember your origins, dweeb."

We grab our things, quickly disassemble, and head to our own little definitions of solitary confinement, also known as our newly designated departments.

The second half of the day takes an entirely different turn.

After break, the customers pile in, and I become overwhelmed with questions about possible furniture combinations, delivery times, and, of course, must endure the occasional advances from the people who I'm sure come to the store just to practice pick up lines.

The day moves by rather quickly nonetheless, and before I know it, it's time to clock out and I make my way out of the doors of FURNISH, finally free, but now anticipating an additional problem, a magical one at that.

Yohan, Lexie, and I previously discussed taking separate Dryve's home, them to grab some things to bring over and create their spaces within our new shared apartment, and me to just take a quick walk-through again to make sure it's really up to par for new room-mates.

Once I finally get home and take a quick look through the apart-ment, I decide now is a great time to check out this digital book of shadows Lexie has created for us to see if it can trigger any ideas of my own that might help us out.

I pull the pink slip of paper out of my pocket, grab my phone, and navigate to DocDrive.

Once I enter the access code, I scroll through the pages. The familiar ones are first: the wishing spell, the warning, the spiral, yeah, yeah, yeah.

Not long after dismissing the spells and enchantments I have be-come so familiar with, I come across new ones, some Lexie has men-tioned, others instantly triggering memories of Madison and what she's revealed about her own journey.

There are instructions for scrying for other witches, absorbing in-formation at an accelerated rate, manipulating technology, spells for constructing magical wards, the details for the glamour Lexie men-tioned, and the ingredients needed to replicate the recipe for the per-fume Madison used to keep us in place when we confronted her in the park.

Amongst all the actual pages, Lexie has sprinkled her own advice based on what we've learned so far from encountering these spells, and once again, it's a smart idea. She never ceases to amaze me.

The perfume.

I scroll back up to where the perfume is listed and read Lexie's note.

Gotcha Bitch. Used to stun an individual, timeframe unknown, reversal listed.

I look through the page and try to dissect the instructions and what would be needed to recreate the mist Madison used on us to keep us frozen in place.

It seems too complicated, and we are literally leaving not long after they get here, so it seems pointless to even consider this as an option.

There goes that idea...

Just as I'm feeling like I've lost all hope of offering anything useful, a notification pops up, revealing a message from Yo-Yo saying he is outside.

I make my way to the front door, unlock it, and let him in.

"Guess I beat Lexie here."

"Yes, you're first."

"Does that mean I get first dibs on choosing a room?" he asks while placing the box he's carrying in his hands on the counter and tossing his bookbag to the side.

"I don't think Lexie will like that very much."

ping

I whip my phone out of my pocket and quickly check my text messages, alerting me of Lexie's arrival.

"Speaking of, she just got here. Perfect timing."

I go to let Lexie in and make my way back to the living room where Yohan has made himself comfortable, sprawled across the couch and scrolling through his phone.

I assume he's going through the pages to think of a plan. I'm pretty sure we all have.

We make small talk as I show Lexie and Yohan the two room options, and they quickly make their choices without hesitation.

Yohan preferred Aeden's because of the look of the accent brick wall. He said it reminds him of a bar, and it was totally punk rock. I don't get it, but hey, to each their own.

Lexie was drawn to Aesher's old room, claiming she liked the large window, as it would provide her healing light during her meditations. Not really my thing. I prefer it dark, but like I said, their choice.

Once the room situation is all figured out, we reconvene in the kitchen around the table to discuss our plan before we head out to the train station. We have about an hour to devise a way to save my brothers and Bash, and time cannot be wasted.

"So, anyone think of anything else that might help? Ella, did you try to prick your finger and see if maybe that would work?"

What is with Lexie wanting to see me in pain lately? She's right, though I probably should have tried.

"I haven't, and before you reach over to slap me again, the thought just slipped my mind. I can try now, though."

"Yes, I think this might really be the answer, or at least the tip we need to figure out where to go from here."

"Okay, give me one sec." I hurry to my room, grab a pin from my sewing kit, and reclaim my seat at the table.

"Okay, here goes nothing." I close my eyes.

"Wait!" Yohan yells, "I have an idea."

I reopen my eyes.

"What?"

"Yeah, what?"

He continues.

"Okay, so remember how we were all able to project the spiral, even though at first we all thought it was what I was meant to do?"

"Yeah, and by the way, why were there four of them?"

"That was Nash, my delusion. He appeared out of nowhere. I guess he really is permanent and sensed I needed help, but that's beside the point. It made me think maybe our powers, the things we wished for, are connected. Maybe we should try to tap into your gift of sight and have a vision together?"

"Okay, now that's an idea, a smart one at that. Different perspectives can help, but how do we even do this?"

"It might sound a bit elementary, but it's the only thing I can think of."

"Maybe we should hold hands while you try to conjure up that vision, prick your finger, and reconnect your hand. Picture all of us having the vision, not just you."

"Well, it didn't really work like that the first time. I kind of went blank, and then I just started seeing things play out before I snapped back."

"Just try. This time, you know what's happening. You know what you want. Will it to be what you desire. We're witches now. Use your will."

"Okay, Mr. Yo-Yo, you get the award for motivational speaker of the day." Lexie pats his back and giggles.

"Alright, let's do this."

Lexie and Yohan connect hands, and I close my eyes, prick my finger, and quickly add my hands to the connection.

My vision goes white, and I try to keep my thoughts focused.

Lexie and Yohan are here with me.

Show me how we save my brothers.

Show me how we save Bash.

The color trickles in, and I know Lex and Yo-Yo are here with me. I can feel their presence.

The sounds changes from static to audible conversation, and we are fully engaged.

I look around the room and notice my brothers leaning on one of the dressing room tables, having a discussion between themselves. I try to listen in, but I am too far away and cannot move. I am not meant to hear whatever they are saying, at least not yet.

I notice Bash dressed as Penny in the corner, sulking while sitting in front of the mirror, looking completely drained. Although his look is disheartening, I can honestly say I am happy to see they're all okay.

That's when I notice the voice behind me, high-pitched and squeaky. I can't turn, I can't move. My only choice is just to listen.

"This isn't working fast enough. We need to move between worlds quickly if we're going to ascend to power. We need the energy to enter the underworld to complete the task."

A second voice replies, a voice I recognize. It's the guy in the video, the one sent from Bash.

"Tell me, Gia, do you know any other ability we can harness to lead us into the underworld undetected other than fearlessness? I don't, and these queens possess that, the ability to stand in front of a crowd and perform as they wish, even though the world may have their biases."

"That is true power, and it comes with a touch of fierceness and strength, I might add, which will only boost our ability to walk between the worlds even more."

"I guess you're right, but won't people come looking for them eventually?"

"Oh my goodness, Gia, we're obviously not going to kill them. Just drain them during their performances to fill the crystals. We already have two complete. We just need a third. There's power in threes, then we deliver them to Patra, she transfers the energy and grants us access to the portal, and boom, we skip the other witches in line and claim our throne."

"We're so bad."

"I know, right?"

They giggle, and it's disturbing.

Just as I feel my skin crawling from the eerie tone their wicked cackles are giving off, my vision fades, and before I know it, I am back around my kitchen table, facing Yohan and Lexie.

Did they see it, too?

Were they really there?

Lexie stands up from her seat around the table, which alerts us to disconnect our hands.

"Patra! I knew there was more to her. I'm going to spiral her ass so hard, I swear!"

"Okay, Lex, first off, that doesn't sound right, and second, we'll worry about her later. Did you hear what they were saying about harnessing energy?"

Yohan quickly offers his opinion.

"Yes, I did. I can't have them using Bash like that. It looks like your brothers might be safe. They only mentioned the queens for their strength and fearlessness, but we should check in with them while we're there. Maybe they have some insight."

"Screw insight. They need to get out of there. Those bitches are evil. They might not be a target now, but who knows what they've got planned next?"

"Your right, well, you guys, are you ready to do this?"

"As ready as I'll ever be."

"Ditto."

Lexie reaches into her pocket, whips out the glamour gloss, and raises it into the air.

Well, get ready to transform you guys.

From regular witches to drag queen sorceresses.

Bixie's Drag Battle, here we come!

Chapter Nineteen

Yohan

I can't believe I'm about to do this.

It's for Bash Yohan.

He'd do it for you.

Besides, it's not that bad.

Pretend it's Halloween, and you're just getting into costume.

Do it for Bash.

I raise the glamour gloss to my lips and try to imagine what type of drag queen I would be if this were really my art form.

She would have to be punk rock, the screw societal norms type.

I take a deep sigh and close my eyes to help ease the anxiety flowing through my body at the thought of what I'm about to do.

I should've hit my Cannapuffy before I attempted this.

I go to press the gloss to my lips, but a hand quickly stops me.

"Yohan, wait." I open my eyes to see Lexie in full drag, displaying a look of concern.

"If it makes you more comfortable, you don't have to do it now; we can wait until we get there. I know it's probably hard for you, but once we're there and you see all the queens, I'm sure it will make you feel more at ease, and you'll be able to blend in."

I breathe a sigh of relief and hand the gloss back to Lexie.

"You've got this, Yohan. We're here to walk you through it, and let me tell you, once you do get in drag, you are going to feel powerful, right Lex?"

"Girl, who are you telling? I feel hashtag sickening. This hair is laid, these nails are fierce, and these heels, well, they speak for themselves."

She struts back and forth through the living room, and I can't help but laugh.

"But honestly, the transformation was a bit lackluster for magic."

"Oh my gosh, right? I was envisioning something like that anime Planet Sisters where they start levitating all dramatically while getting into costume with glitter dust and living their best lives."

"Same, but hey, on the upside, we're absolutely gorgeous."

"Totes."

I must admit, I do see the boost in confidence in them, and I could definitely use that right about now, but it's just so different to me that I think I'd rather wait, wait until I have the inspiration, wait until I see Bash.

"Okay, you guys, let's get out of here. We need to catch this train and be on our way, Haus of Ascension, to the rescue."

"Ella, I swear, if you don't cut the shit, I'm going to end up slapping you again, and this time, it won't be to trigger a vision."

I chuckle as we make our way out of the door of our apartment, Lexie and Ella taking the lead, their heels clicking as we march towards our Dryve, waiting to take us on our next magical endeavor.

The Dryve ride is quiet, and I can tell the driver is taken aback by the outfits Lexie and Ella are now wearing.

It might be Aella's blue Mohawk or Lexie's dramatic makeup, but whatever it is, it keeps making her peek into the rearview, and we can tell she has a hidden opinion.

The train station isn't too far from our apartment, which is a good thing because even though I'm not taking part in the drag glamour for now, our driver's awkward energy was a bit off, so I'm pretty sure the girls are just as enthusiastic about exiting her car as I am.

We make it just in time to hop on the train heading to Fairview, and that's when I start to feel guilty that I didn't choose to participate from the beginning.

I can hear the comments as we make our way to our seats, and if we're a team, I should be here with them, supporting them, doing this with them.

We take our seats, and I can't help but offer up an apology because this is a lot, and Lex and Ella are getting the brunt of it.

"You guys, I'm sorry. I should've done it, too. I don't feel..."

"Yo-Yo, stop. This is life; people won't like everything you do, and Ella and I find it quite humorous, really. I mean, who are we really hurting by being fabulous?"

"Yeah, fashion is a form of self-expression. If they don't like my display, they can avert their eyes elsewhere." She yells as she snaps her fingers dramatically.

"Ella, see, this is the attitude I was trying to tell you that we need to have earlier, especially with all this crazy stuff happening. I don't know where it's coming from, but I like it."

"I think it's the glamour. My thoughts are all over the place. It's hard to stay quiet. I want to read a bitch for filth!"

"Yass! Read her! Drag her!" Lexie covers her mouth.

She drops her hands back to her lap, looks away, and fidgets with her skirt. "Yeah, I see what you mean."

I can't help but laugh.

The train ride is long, but our conversation makes it go by quickly. The humor that the glamour has gifted Lexie and Ella with is astronomical, not that they weren't funny before, but this, this is like a whole new level of comical genius, has been unlocked.

When the train finally reaches Fairview, we exit the station and order a Dryve.

God, I wish one of us had a car.

That would make things so much easier.

I try to think about our train ride and how much fun Lexie and Ella were having with their newly discovered personalities.

Am I really ready, though?

I can wait; I still have time.

I know Bash will be the one to give me the push I need to try something new.

I'm doing this for him.

My thoughts are interrupted by the arrival of our Dryve, and we pile into the back of our driver's car, finally on our way to our last stop.

The anxiety is building up. I reach into my pocket and hold on to my Cannapuffy for a bit of comfort.

"It's okay, Yo-Yo, plus I think I have a better plan," Ella says as she places her hand on my shoulder with a squeeze in what I assume is her attempt to provide some consolation.

It works, and I am thankful.

We finally pull up to where Bixie's is being filmed, and I must admit the awe of it all has me utterly stunned. We're not even inside yet, and I can hear the crowd cheering and the music blasting, but above all, I can literally feel the energy emanating from the building.

It's an energy of celebration.

The thought of celebrating being different gives me the boost I need. I think of all the things I've been through, the things I've tried to fight, the things I've tried to hide. I think of Bash.

I'm doing this for him.

"Okay, guys, I'm ready. Hand me the gloss."

"Okay, but before I do, I think we could all use a touch-up." Lexie winks at us and pulls her hairbrush out of her bag, which I know is concealing Ms. Cookie Dough.

"Well, a little primping before a performance is just absolutely necessary, isn't it?" Ella winks back.

We find a spot across the street from the auditorium. I take hits from my Cannapuffy for confidence as we pass the hairbrush around and review our plan.

"So, I think our best bet is to use the tech binding technique that Madison used on us. It's fairly simple: point our phones and use the words of power. I think we should use hers. I have no idea what Sudo Su means, but I kind of like it."

"But don't you think we'll get noticed if we just walk up to security and wrap them in a digital text string? If our goal is going incognito, this will blow our cover."

"Well, that brings me back to the idea I mentioned earlier."

Ella takes a gulp of whiskey and proceeds to explain.

"Yo-Yo, I know you're uncomfortable getting into drag, and maybe you don't have to. What if you use the glamour to mimic the identity of a security guard to get us in?"

"God, Ella, that's so smart. Why didn't I think of that?"

Why didn't I?

I mean, it makes sense.

"Okay, sounds like a plan." I take one last hit from my Cannapuffy. "Ready?"

"Ready."

"Let's do this!"

Lexie hands me the glamour gloss, I close my eyes and think of the security guard we spotted when we exited our Dryve.

I try to envision that my glamour is believable, that I am escorting Ella and Lexie into the drag battle.

I open my eyes to find Ella and Lexie staring jaws dropped and just waiting to say something.

"Whoa, Yohan, I mean, you were cute before, but wow, that uniform, and I mean seriously, did you have to envision that body? I mean, I'm no hater, but wow." Lexie reaches into her bag and hands me her Purr Kittie compact.

I snatch the compact from her excitedly.

"Sorry."

"No, no, do you boo, boo."

I prop open the compact to take a look and position it at different angles to see the new me. She is right.

I am EVERYTHING.

What the hell, it's the glamour.

I don't think like this.

At least not about myself.

Whatever the case may be, I am ready.

I take the lead as we approach the front entrance, and I can't help but notice my anxiety is completely gone. I feel confident, as confident as I have ever been.

I might need to make a tube for myself, not that I want to change who I am, but maybe it can add some confidence to the person I already am so I can become who I really want to be.

"Bro, they were supposed to be in an hour ago for their perfor-mance. They're new. They got lost." I gesture toward Ella and Lexie.

"I don't get paid to know details; just take them where they need to be before Bixie has a fit and we lose our jobs." The guard replies, clearly annoyed.

I choose not to respond and proceed towards the door.

I try to pull it open, but it's locked.

Shit.

Before I can process what's happening, the guard reaches over and scans his badge across the reader, unlocking the door.

"Freaking temps, I swear." He huffs.

The three of us enter the door, and the music and cheering are so loud it causes my head to spin. We are darting our eyes to every corner of the building so quickly that I'm sure anyone observing would most likely describe us as a small herd of deer stuck in headlights.

It's not long before another guard approaches us.

"Dude, what are you doing?"

I try to think fast.

"Uh, this is Sue She and Moe Hawk." I gesture toward Ella and Lexie.

"I noticed they were missing, and I've been looking everywhere for them... I found them outside. Looks like the stress was getting to them, and they just needed to step out and get some air."

"Okay, I don't need the details. They should be in the dressing room. The queens wait to be called to the stage from the dressing room. If they miss their cue, Bixie will go ape shit."

I quickly think of a reply.

"Yeah, I'm new. I was just trying to get them there," I respond nervously.

He mutters under his breath, "Freaking temps."

I can hear Lexie and Ella giggling in the background.

Alex, the guard, leads us through the back to a long hallway, which I assume is directly behind the stage because now the music is louder, and the speakers' vibration is highly intense.

He points to a door at the end of a hallway marked with a large gold star.

"Get them in there to get ready. You can handle that, can't you? The door is right there, or will you get lost again?"

"I got it, Alex."

"Okay, good. I've got other things to do." He says as he walks away, pulling his phone out of his pocket.

I breathe a sigh of relief.

"Yo-Yo, you did it! Very convincing."

"Very." Ella agrees.

"Okay, you guys, you ready?" Ella asks, while adjusting her outfit.

"Not just yet. Can I get the gloss?"

Lexie looks at me, puzzled.

"Aww, Lex, he wants to do it for Bash."

"Aww." She hands me the gloss and I redden.

You can do this.

I close my eyes and envision the queen I thought of before, the punk rock, screw the system, badass that I know I can be.

I swipe the gloss across my lips and open my eyes.

"Oh my God, Yo-Yo, you are gorgeous."

"Absolutely stunning."

I reach my hand out toward Lexie, and without a word, she passes her compact to me.

I can't believe what I'm seeing, and I must admit I kind of like it, and I get what they mean. I do feel powerful.

I stare in awe at my rainbow hair, my black makeup with subtle touches of color sprinkled throughout its placement, and the glitter strategically placed on my left cheek in the form of a spiral.

I am wearing the true essence of who I am.

For the first time, I am not creating art.

I am art.

Living, breathing art.

"Let's save the people that are important to us. Haus of Ascension, here we go." I take the lead as I stomp my heels towards the door.

The walk down the hall seems never-ending as we strut to save our friends and our family.

When we finally reach the door, and I place my hand on the handle, the only thoughts that take over my mind are about him.

I can't wait to see him.

I can't wait to see Bash.

CHAPTER TWENTY

Yohan

*W*ow
I can't believe what I'm seeing.

Talk about magic. This place is screaming art and talent.

You can feel their craft's creativity through the energy resonating in the room.

Before I can take too much time to look around and really take in the artistic expression of the queens, my eyes instantly dart to him.

I am focused on Bash.

The emotions rush through me instantaneously.

I can't believe we're here.

I'm going to do it.

This time, I'm going to save him.

It's like I'm frozen in place. The feeling never changes. We've only seen each other in person a few times, because of me constantly moving, but every time feels like the first because there is just an unspoken understanding between us, one that can't ever be replaced.

It doesn't take long before my awe is interrupted by one of the queens stationed at her makeup table, and by her facial expression; she is not at all excited to see us.

She addresses us, verifying my assumption.

"New queens? Seriously? How are you already in full drag? How did you get separate dressing rooms? You're clearly not returning competitors. I haven't seen you on any previous seasons, and trust me, I've done my research, honey."

The queen stands and puts her hand on her hip, eyes exploring the three of us curiously from head to toe.

Lexie quickly replies.

"We're contractually obligated to keep the secrets of Bixie's twists for the show under wraps for the time being."

"I call bullshit!" another queen calls out from her place in the dressing room.

My eyes dart back toward her, then Bash, who is sitting at his station, awkwardly quiet, observing but detached and disconnected.

Don't worry, Bash, I'm here to set you free.

We just need to play this smart. We've come this far; we can't blow it now.

A third queen adds her input to the conversation.

"Now, ladies, there's an easy way to solve this."

She stands and makes her way toward the door.

"I'll just make a brief call to production. They shouldn't have a problem just verifying..."

"Sudo Su."

The queen drops to the floor with a screech as Lexie's digital text string binds her in place, triggering shrieks and gasps from the rest of the room.

"I didn't want to do that, but you guys are in trouble. We're here to help. I can't have you alerting the people running all of this. They are your enemies, not us."

"Also, don't try anything slick. The three of us are capable of way more than you think. Let us help you."

The queen, currently bound by Lexie's magic, lets out a grunt, and I feel bad for her. I remember how painful it was when Madison pinned us to the Elm tree the other night. I motion to Lexie to ease up on her a bit.

She points her phone toward the queen. "Sudo Su, loosen."

The queen lets out an exasperated breath.

"Who are you guys?" Bash speaks for the first time since we've been here, and it's refreshing to hear his voice.

Lexie and Ella both look at me and smile.

It's clearly my turn to take center stage.

I take a deep breath, and I feel my eyes start to water. "Your unannounced visitor has arrived."

I see the feelings making their way through his expressions, his eyes confused and emotional, but then he does something I'm sure he hasn't been able to do genuinely in the past few days.

He smiles.

"Yo-Yo, is it really you?"

"It is, and I'm here to save you, and maybe after, we can pick out that new desk you mentioned."

He giggles. "I never thought I'd see you in makeup, much less full drag."

"I guess I'm trying something new. I have to say I see why you like it so much." I attempt to emulate one of Lexie's signature hair flips, but by the roar of his laughter, I can tell it was a failure.

"How do we even know we can trust you guys? And what is happening? What are you saving us from exactly?" the bound queen asks.

I turn to Lexie, whose eyes are now surveying the room, most likely looking for something to help prove our case.

"Sudo Su reverse."

My attention moves over to Ella, who has her phone pointed at the intercom adhered to the wall next to the door we entered through, and the room goes quiet as we eavesdrop on the conversation.

It is the conversation from our shared vision. We study the queens as they take in the information we already know.

While the conversation plays out, I can't help but keep my gaze focused on Ella.

Why isn't she confronting her brothers?

Can they tell it's her under the glamour?

What is going through her head?

They are oddly quiet and just taking this all in.

Are they in on it?

No, they would've alerted someone.

What is going on?

"Sudo Su quiet." She silences the intercom.

"Believe us now?"

The queens exchange glances with each other, all clearly driven by fear and curiosity, but it's not long before the silence is broken.

"Harvesting our energy? Walking between worlds? What is going on? What is this? Who are you guys?"

"Penny, who are they?" the bound queen asks frantically, leading the others to direct their attention to Bash.

"Yo-Yo is my good friend, and anything he says I trust, he's here to help. I reached out to him because I overheard a conversation between Gia and Cody about magic and draining our energy."

"We need to listen to him."

My heart grows warm, and I can't tell if it's from his confidence in me or Nash's lingering words that have been living in my head ever since they first left his lips.

"Why is my name so similar to the boy you've been trying to save? The one you're afraid you might have feelings for?"

My thought process is quickly interrupted by Lexie's interjection.

"We obviously can't all go storming out of here. If Cody and Gia are as powerful as they claim to be, they must have something up their sleeves. We'll start with Bash, Aeden, and Aesher. We'll be back for you guys, and quickly, I promise."

"How do you know our names?" One of Ella's brothers asks, and I'm unclear which one is speaking because the resemblance is uncanny.

"We'll start with Bash and just Bash," Ella responds firmly, completely ignoring her brother's question.

She points her phone toward the bound queen. "Sudo Su, free."

"Let's go."

I gesture toward Bash, signaling him to come along with us. He quickly grabs his things, and we make our way out of the door.

We make it halfway down the hall when I realize that if we're going to get out of here unnoticed, we probably shouldn't be in total drag.

"Lexie, the glamour gloss."

We take turns using the gloss to return to our usual selves. I can see the look in Bash's eyes waver between curiosity and excitement, and when it's finally his turn to have a taste of magic, I'm happy that his first experience is here with me in this moment.

Don't be nervous, it's Bash, your person.

I reach out my hand, and he locks his hand into mine as if by instinct.

"Aww so cute."

"Super cute."

We both chuckle at Lexie and Ella's comment, but the time is ticking by, and we need to get out of here, so I try to get as serious as possible so I can walk Bash through this.

"Okay, it's simple. I will you to use this magic, Bash. Just close your eyes and envision you, the real you."

He closes his eyes and uses his free hand to apply the gloss, and I watch his transformation.

It's him, the real him, the Bash who loves makeup.

"Well, clearly, we need better imaginations because your face is beat for the gods!"

"Yeah, so much for Moe Hawk and Sue She. They have been slayed and not the good kind."

We all laugh and continue to make our exit. With all the chuckling and joking we were doing on the way out, it's a miracle we escaped undetected, but now that we have, there's just one more thing I need to do.

"Do you guys think I could have a minute? I use my eyes to gesture toward Bash."

"Of course," Lexie responds while giggling, grabbing Ella's arm, and guiding her across the street.

"Hey, Bash," I say nervously, glancing at the ground.

He chuckles. "Hey, Yohan, what's up?"

I know he doesn't want to talk about it, but I have to know. I have to let him know I'm here for him, too, just like he's always here for me.

"What happened to you that night? The night we were talking, and you were upset."

I see his face change, and I feel like I made the biggest mistake by asking him this, but I need to know.

"It's stupid, but you went through all this to save me, so I do owe you an explanation."

"A group of guys approached me, they started harassing me because I was wearing makeup, and that's something I've grown used to, even though I know it shouldn't be okay, but it's more the things they were saying, Yohan."

"They made me feel like I'm not even human, like I'm a mistake, that everything I love is wrong. I don't know why, but it got to me. If there's one thing this whole experience has taught me, it's that once you find your tribe, other people like you, or even other people who just accept you, focus on that, and things will be okay."

I fight back the emotion.

"Bash, not only are you human, but you are my favorite human. If you could only see how amazing you truly are from my perspective, you would never feel out of place again."

The air tightens, and we grow silent, bashfully looking into each other's eyes occasionally. Yet, before this moment ends, I have something I need to say.

I break the silence.

"So, I was thinking... and uh, I've been thinking a lot lately actually, um, about... about you."

He smiles.

"I've been thinking a lot about you too, Yo-Yo, and thank you for saving me. You're an amazing friend, someone I know I can count on when things get rough."

He chuckles, and that's when I hear it.

That voice that has become too familiar.

It's Nash.

"Just go for it. You'll never know if you don't try. Isn't this what you want? True love?"

I try to ignore him and not respond so I don't look like a crazy person talking to myself.

I try to keep on my train of thought with Bash even though my anxiety is beyond through the roof right now.

I just have to say it.

"I've been thinking about more... maybe us being more?"

That was stupid. God, Yohan, get it together.

This time, I cannot read his face. It's stiff, there's no emotion, no inclination of what's coming next, and my heart flutters with antici-pation.

I am afraid.

After what seems like forever, he finally responds.

"I can't lie, Yohan. I've thought about it too, so many times over the years. You are so perfect in my eyes, so talented, so attractive, so surprising and mysterious."

I grow warm, and I know I'm turning red.

"But..."

My heart sinks.

"I don't want to ruin us." He motions between us with his pointer fingers, clearly referring to our connection.

Our connection as friends.

He wants friendship and only friendship, and I don't know how to process it after being so vulnerable.

"It's not like we won't still be here for each other. Some relation-ships, you know, they end, but the best of friendships, they usually don't."

"I just don't want to lose you."

"You're right. I'm sorry that was stupid."

I wipe away the tears that escaped.

"It wasn't, Yohan. I'm..."

I cut him off.

I don't want to hear anything else.

I need time to process it all.

"Do you want to catch a Dryve with us, or are you heading out on your own?"

"Uh, I should, uh, probably catch my own, message me later?"

"Sure." He reaches out for a hug, but I quickly move my body in decline and make my way to the other side of the street where the people who do love me are waiting.

"So, how'd it go?" Lexie asks eagerly, bouncing up and down.

"Can we just not talk about it and order a Dryve?"

"Sure, we'll talk when you are ready, if you want."

"Thanks."

She orders the Dryve, and we sit huddled on the curb, waiting for it to arrive. With all the things going on with Bash, I forgot there's one question I still have.

"Hey, Ella, what happened to saving your brothers? Why did you say they couldn't come?"

She clears her throat, and Lexie puts her arm around her shoulders to comfort her.

I can tell that whatever she's about to say is making her upset.

"Well, Yo-Yo, as I was telling Lexie, this new psychic ability is weird."

"Me and my brothers have always had a connection, this inner knowing with each other, and when I was in the room with them, something felt off."

"It's like they knew what was happening and didn't care, like they were thirsty for power, like they knew it was me in drag and they wouldn't get hurt. I honestly don't know what they knew, but it felt evil."

"I don't know if the wish affected them, or they were offered an invitation to practice magic themselves, I really don't know. Whatever it is, it scares me because this journey that we're on now comes with two sides, there's us, then the opposing, and I really don't want to end up going against my brothers."

It's hard to hear what she's telling me, and I'm so overwhelmed with emotion that all I can do is let her know that we're all here for each other on this journey to wherever the hell we're going for whatever reason.

Lexie does her best to reassure her she has her back, too, which I'm sure she already knows, but even when you know something, sometimes it's still good to hear it.

We lighten up the conversation by scrolling through pages of our digital book of shadows and adding our own little comments while we wait for our Dryve.

Lexie leaves a note saying to be sure to look at makeup tips before attempting to use the glamour gloss. Ella creates a page about shared visions, and I add to the page of the spiral warning that it comes along with an annoying but attractive imaginary friend.

The Dryve finally approaches, and we make our way in.

The ride is quiet. I'm pretty sure we're all exhausted from this long day, and I can't wait just to decompress and think things through.

When I finally reach my soon-to-be old apartment, I make my way to my room and pack up the last of the items I'm taking with me before I officially call it a night.

As I pack the memories away in boxes, I can honestly say that I'm excited but also sad that I'll be away from my dad. We've always been there for each other, but it seems like my life is transforming, and this is just another change I need to push through.

The conversation with him about moving went better than expected. For once, he seemed genuinely proud of me for taking my life into my own hands and going for something that I want. He's always been supportive, and I'm glad I'm making him proud.

I keep the words he said to me close to my heart.

Now you don't have only one home. You have two. You're always welcome to come back.

Once everything is stacked neatly in the corner and I can finally take a breather, I lay on my bed and try to process what I've been through so far.

It's not Bash.

He's not my soul mate.

Nash isn't real.

I'm finally going to be on my own.

The battle with Madison is finally over.

I can't believe it's real.

Magic is real.

Chapter Twenty-One

Lexie

IT'S FUNNY HOW THINGS never really go the way anyone plans. No matter how many stars you send your wishes or how hard you try to influence your reality, things seem to work out the way they are destined to.

As I sit back in my newly half-decorated room, I replay the events that have happened over the past couple of days: receiving that crazy email, meeting Yohan, and my overall crazy journey with magic.

Even though it has been a few days since our last magical adventure, I can't help but wonder if my life will ever be the same or if I'm stuck on this crazy journey through the unknown, searching for something I'm not even sure I really want to find or even desire.

All I really know is that we're in it deep now, and there's no turning back, or if there is, we just haven't found it yet, not that we have really been searching.

Working at FURNISH has continued to be exhausting, and as I prop myself off my bed and into the living room, the guilt floods over me about how Xyla must feel now that I am out of the house and on my own.

I must admit I do feel like I have been neglecting her a bit since I've been so busy trying to figure all of this out, but I intend on keeping close to her because I know she looks up to me, and that's a bond I just can't afford to lose.

Maybe I'll schedule a mystery movie night here.
She'd like that.

I gaze around the living room at my new living space, and my eyes instantly dart to our cute little glass case propped against the wall.

Yo-Yo, Ella, and I spent the past couple of days preparing things from our digital grimoire and stacking them on shelves to prepare for what comes next.

Tubes of glamour gloss, bottles of Gotcha Bitch, and various items such as crystals and tarot cards are among the things on display in our magical collection.

I feel a sense of pride when I look at all the things we've curated and acquired, but once again, the guilt is triggered because these items carry memories of our journey so far, and within that journey lies broken promises.

We didn't have time to make it back to rescue the queens, not because we didn't want to, but because we couldn't collectively think of a logical plan.

After a lengthy discussion, we decided it might be better to try to recover the crystals to restore the energy that was taken from them.

The decision seemed to make sense. After all, Gia and Cody didn't intend to kill them, so in retrospect, they will be safe until we can offer help, hopefully with more expertise.

Our experience of attempting to rescue the queens came with some clarification on some issues for both Yohan and Ella, but that new-found clarification caused new questions to arise.

Ella hasn't tried to contact her brothers since Bixie's but has attempted to consult the cards with no obvious answers as to what Aedan and Aesher are really up to.

On the other hand, Yohan finally told me about what happened between him and Bash but has been questioning if the effects of the crystals might have influenced Bash's response to him because, according to him, a piece of Bash might have been missing.

His fearlessness.

He hasn't tried to contact him since, but he's slowly healing, and I figure he just needs time.

With all these thoughts flowing through my mind, I make my way to my favorite spot on the sofa, power on the TV, and start scrolling through stations, trying to find something to distract me while I wait for our final delivery from FURNISH to arrive.

God, I can't wait for that new body pillow.

And those accent lamps are super cute.

Maybe I should've gone with gold?

My thought process is quickly interrupted by Ella clumsily bursting through the door.

"Girl, I went to two different stores. They are totally out of cookie dough whiskey. You're going to put the distillery out of business! I got gingerbread. You're just going to have to deal."

"Yuck."

She tosses the bottle of whiskey on the sofa next to me and makes her way to the bathroom door.

Knock Knock

"Oh my God, Yo-Yo, you've been in there before I even left. What are you doing? You better not be in there getting freaky with your delusion! We all have to use that bathroom, you know! Hurry up, I have to pee!"

I can't help but giggle.

Yohan opens the door slowly, and I notice something different about him. His patch of hair in the front that was once blue is now an eye-catching hot pink, and I like it.

I like it a lot.

"What do you guys think?"

"Loves it, now move. I have to pee." Ella rushes into the bathroom and slams the door.

"I totally love it. I have to admit I will miss the blue, though, but may I ask what inspired this fashionable change?"

I wiggle the whiskey bottle in the air, and he takes a seat next to me.

"I don't know, I just wanted something new, and it's kind of a nod to you guys, to us, to the Haus of Ascension, and all the things we've been through so far, I think if I had to choose a color for it, it would be pink."

Ella comes out of the bathroom and sits beside us on the sofa.

"Definitely pink." We all giggle.

We decide to watch a Rom-Com, it's kind of become our thing, while we pass around the bottle of gingerbread whiskey, which I abhor but indulge in.

"That's it. I'm ordering my whiskey online from now on."

"Yeah, this is horrible."

"That's an understatement."

Knock Knock

"Omg! Our delivery it's finally here!"

I jump off the couch, belly full of whiskey, and make my way to the front door of our apartment, ready to get my new items and finish decorating my space.

Swinging open the door enthusiastically ready to greet the delivery guy, my excitement quickly turns to confusion when no one is there.

I look to the floor and see a strange stuffed creature holding an envelope marked Eat Your Heart Out.

Patra.

I'm not Yohan.

I'm not as patient.

I pick up the creepy stuffed creature, grab the envelope, rip it open, and begin to read the note inside.

Hello,

You were warned.

Now, not only are you uninvited, but you have made an enemy.

I tried to be kind.

I'm pretty sure we'll be seeing each other soon.

For now, I leave you my Ju-Ju.

They'll keep a close eye on you.

Until we meet again.

-Patra, the vampire queen.

She's got the wrong one.

I march the plush to the trash, shove it in, and close the lid.

I return to the front porch where the plush is now sitting, once again where I initially found it.

WTF

I don't even have the energy for this right now.

I shake off my nerves, knowing it's time for battle.

Patra, you have absolutely no idea who you're playing with.

I scream through the front door.

"Yohan, get your delusional ass out here!"

"Ella, grab and fill the hairbrush!"

"These vampires got us all the way effed up!"

Eat Your
Heart Out